VENGEANCE IS MINE

A DARK ROMANCE

MAFIA BRIDES

LEE SAVINO

FREE BOOK

My dark lumberjack romance, Beauty & the Lumberjacks, is free right now for newsletter subscribers

Grab it here: https://BookHip.com/WZLTMQX

Beauty & the Lumberjacks

After this logging season, I'm never having sex again. Because: *reasons*.

But first, I have a gig earning room and board and ten thousand dollars by 'entertaining' eight lumberjacks. **Eight strong and strapping Paul Bunyan types, big enough to break me in two.**

There's Lincoln, the leader, the stern, silent type...

Jagger, the Kurt Cobain look-alike, with a soul full of music and rockstar moves...

Elon & Oren, ginger twins who share everything...

Saint, the quiet genius with a monster in his pants...

Roy and Tommy, who just want to watch...

And Mason, who hates me and won't say why, but on his night tries to break me with pleasure...

They own me: body, mind and orgasms.

But when they discover my secret—the reason I'm hiding from the world—everything changes.

VENGEANCE IS MINE

"They said I could choose my reward. I choose you."

It was a simple job: go to a wedding. Execute the groom.

Then I saw the bride, wearing a mountain of white satin, her lacy veil now spattered with blood.

Instead of running away screaming like the rest of the wedding party, she raised her chin and stared at me, a challenge in her dark eyes. I felt a flicker of feeling in my cold, dark heart...

Then she shot me. And I knew...

I had to make her mine.

Vengeance is Mine is a stand alone dark romance with adult themes, starring an obsessed hitman, a heroine bent on vengeance, and an HEA (happily ever after).

“OMG!!! Victor and Lula are the hottest couple ever! And I read a lot of erotic books but this one. Wow! I couldn’t put it down it just called to me on a primal level. I’ve always loved Lee Savino’s stories but this one is exceptional!”

“Hot and punishing as well as digging deep into the soul. I loved it.”

“Holy yowza, this grabs you by the throat right in the beginning and doesn’t let go! (You’ll get it when you read it 😉). And read it you must!! This was dark & smoldering, dangerous all around!! Lula is intelligent and lethal. And Victor, wow, he’s vicious in many ways. Controlling. And HOT. But you also get the other side of him with Lula. And it’s everything!”

“Victor takes what he wants and he wants Lula.”

“It comes with a paragraph of trigger warnings. Mind. Them. She’s not kidding.”

CONTENT WARNINGS

Murder, death of a beloved parent (in the past), abduction/seduction, non- and dubious consent, sensory deprivation and torture, cage confinement, knife play, blood play, butt stuff, decapitation.

Find the Vengeance is Mine playlist on Spotify.

1

L*ula*

THE AIR at the altar of the church is thick and heavy, compressed from decades of Sunday sermons. It smells like pompous preaching and unanswered prayers, with an aftertaste of stale lemony furniture polish. The only sounds are the occasional coughs and creaks from guests shifting in the wooden pews.

Under the crime against fashion that is my wedding gown, I shift from foot to foot. Tacky white satin heels pinch my feet, and the once rich red carpet I'm standing on has faded to an anemic pink, too thin to cushion anything. My head is completely shrouded by the traditional veil, so no one can see my resting bitch face.

My groom, David, stands at my side. A snowfall of dandruff dusts the shoulders of his dark suit, and his nostrils are dusted white from the cocaine habit he's hoping to hide.

Every few seconds, his eyes slide towards me, checking to make sure I'm still beside him. When he sees that I am, he blinks, and his dull brown eyes brighten like he can't believe his luck. As far as he's concerned, I'm a dream girl he conjured from his fantasies, sleek and elegant and soft-spoken. . . and way, way out of his league. Yet willing, nay insisting, we marry. A mythical creature, like a unicorn. Blink, and I'll disappear.

If I'm lucky, all the guests will be wondering how he snared me, and not how whirlwind our courtship was or why the bride's side of the church is completely empty.

The organ notes die with a sound like an accordion falling down the stairs. The minister clears his throat.

"Dearly beloved," he intones. I can smell his halitosis from here.

David's great aunt Eunice, his only living relative, booked this venue. In the interest of speed, I let her plan everything except my dress. She dug the veil I'm wearing out of storage and ordered the peonies in my bouquet. I told her I was allergic to peonies. She either didn't care or did it on purpose. She thinks there's something off about me, about this whole wedding.

For a fossil, Eunice is pretty sharp. She senses a con, but her grand nephew is properly fooled. As far as he's concerned, I'm his true love. I've sold the image of a soft-spoken, smitten virgin so well, I'm impressed with myself. I deserve an acting reward for how well I've pretended his touch doesn't make my skin crawl.

Eunice glares at me from the front pew, and I freeze my fidgeting until I resemble a mannequin in a bridal shop window, stiff and swathed in white. I chose my dress. It's huge and puffy with yards of itchy crinoline and lace. Perfect for my plan.

The minister is droning on about love and commitment and all the things that don't apply to this marriage. I want to tell him to hurry up. The sooner I'm married, the sooner I can roofie my groom and go hunting for the quarry I really want. *Stephanos.*

We're halfway through the most boring ceremony in the world when the bang of doors opening echoes from the foyer to the altar. The minister coughs and falls silent, fumbling in his train of thought. The pews creak as curious guests turn as one to investigate.

A late arrival? I remain staring at the minister, ignoring the interruption. It's only when David turns and frowns, his pasty skin blanching further, that I turn, too.

A man prowls up the aisle from the back of the church, wearing a dark suit and a viper's smile. He has white blond hair, close-cropped to his head. Shadows lie in the hollows under his eyes and cheekbones. The sleek suit obscures the breadth of his shoulders and the athleticism of the powerful body underneath.

A jolt runs through me. His features are perfect, so perfect, it hurts to look at him. Judging from the way women in the audience suck in a breath, I'm not the only one who thinks so. But I might be the only one who notices the feral tilt to his smile and the intense light in his eyes. He looks more hungry than happy. Expectant.

Years of instincts honed from being around dangerous men tell me this man belongs in their ranks.

The church is quiet, the only sound a candle guttering out in its candelabra. Eunice has turned her glare to the latecomer, pressing her lips together until they're white. Whoever this is, she either disapproves of him, his interruption, or both.

Is this the best man? He's striding straight to the altar toward us like an oncoming storm.

And the closer he gets, the taller he looms. He's taller than David, who towers over me.

He doesn't spare me a glance but steps smoothly up to David, who licks his lips, obviously unsure how to respond.

The newcomer murmurs, "Stefanos sends his regards." With practiced grace, he pulls David into a one-armed hug, his right arm clamping around David's shoulders while his left arm folds between them.

In the man's embrace, David's body jerks hard, and a half gasp, half gurgle escapes his parted lips. The intruder releases David and steps back. Metal flashes between the dark suits.

David folds forwards, a bright spurt of cartoonishly red blood spurting from his chest. The ketchup-colored liquid spatters my veil, and the white satin of my gown soaks up the droplets.

The intruder stands aside, a hint of amusement in his serpentine smile. David crashes to the floor, choking on his own blood.

My ears are ringing. Someone is screaming, and there are panicked cries and scrambling feet in the pews. The chaplain's Bible thuds onto the ancient carpet. His shoes make no sound as he flees, leaving me as the only witness to watch the light fade from David's eyes.

Blood speckles David's gray face and soaks his white shirt. The knife got him in the heart. That's not an easy strike. It takes force to push a blade through someone's ribs, through the pericardium, and into the beating, vital organ. And this man did it with the coolness of someone hugging a brother to congratulate him on his wedding day.

There's not going to be a wedding, not anymore. The

guests are gone, fleeing what they can rightly guess is a mob execution. A metallic taste is in my mouth, and my empty stomach is roiling. The echo of slammed doors dies away, and I stand speckled with my betrothed's blood, my plan for vengeance dying at my feet.

How am I going to get close to Stephanos now? David was the closest tie I had. Except...

Stephanos sends his regards.

Stephanos ordered this hit. I've made a study of the top tier of his gang, and I don't recognize this ice-eyed hitman. In a rustle of satin, I turn to face him.

Up close, his beauty is sharp and striking. He's beautiful like a well-balanced knife is beautiful. In the way a Sig Sauer pistol or a F-22 Raptor is beautiful. Stunning and deadly.

The killer still hasn't looked at me. I might as well be an object on the altar—a candelabra or a tablecloth—for all the attention he's paid me. If this was a hit on my life, if I was the actual target, he would've made his move by now.

Right?

That smug curve to his lips tells me he likes killing and the thrill of the hunt. Everything in me screams to run or fight.

Adrenaline floods my veins. My fingers flex, aching to reach for a weapon. But I hold the rest of me still, waiting to make my choice. Each second, I gather more information and expand my choices.

The hitman finally looks at me, and his blue eyes snag on my lips. I painted them red, a color bright enough to be seen under the stupid veil. His gaze trolls up and down my body, taking in my stained gown and the thick shroud over my features. There's no flicker of recognition on his face.

If the hitman doesn't know me, does he just see a bride

standing over her love, too shocked to scream? I probably should run or cry. I've spent too much time calculating my next moves. I need to play my part.

But those arctic eyes freeze me. His head cocks to the side, and for a moment, I think he'll speak.

But he doesn't. What he does is kneel to check the dead man's eyes for proof of life. With cruel casualness, he wipes his blade clean on David's tuxedo pant leg. Then he rises, gives me a smile, and strolls back the way he came.

The pool of David's blood has reached my foot. I back away, cataloging my emotions. Horror. Annoyance. A resigned sort of calm.

I toss the bouquet of peonies into the closest pew, pick up my dress and stride away. Toward the front of the church, not the back. I don't want to be caught in the tangle of David's friends and his lone relative, none of whom had the wherewithal to stand strong.

David was my way to get Stephanos. I had hoped Stephanos would show up at the wedding so I could execute him during the reception. Barring that, I intended to spend my 'honeymoon' setting a trap and springing it.

I'll need more than luck to get so close again. If my plan is going to work, I'll need a new way in. Soon, immediately, before my cousin Royal tracks me down. He's the head of the Regis *Famiglia* now and has never approved of my quest for vengeance.

Stephanos sends his regards. Ironically, my best lead is the blond hitman. I shiver as I think of him. Those piercing eyes, that powerful frame. So beautiful and so cold.

I rub my chest and automatically grasp the delicate necklace at my throat, a tiny sword that rests between my breasts. I kiss the small pommel for good luck and tuck it back into place.

I stride out of the church, ready to call a cab and head to a safe house for a change of clothes and a glass of whiskey while I rework my plan. Marrying David was supposed to be the beginning of the end. Now, I'm back where I started. And I look like a damn runaway bride. A runaway bride covered in blood spatter.

Fuck my life.

I don't get more than a few steps out the door before someone seizes me from behind, immobilizing me in strong arms. I see a glint of metal, and in a smooth, practiced move, my attacker raises a knife past my blood-speckled bodice to rest at my throat.

"Not so fast, beautiful," the hitman rasps in my ear. "You're coming with me."

2

V*ictor*

The bride is a warm bundle in my arms, if not exactly willing. Her feet drag, but she doesn't put up a fight as I bundle her into the backseat of the waiting car. This job came with a driver, but there's a divider between him and the backseat. I'll have plenty of privacy to play with my new toy.

She settles into the car seat beside me, filling the space with mounds and mounds of white satin. A bride on her wedding day, representing love and innocence and purity and all the things I've never experienced. All the things the world withholds from a soulless man like me.

But now I have her in my clutches. My blood heats, and I have to force myself to slow down, remain cool and in control. She is a prize like no other. A triumph I wish to savor as long as possible.

The car pulls away from the curb, and the bride's back hits the seat. Her chest rises and falls rapidly, making the delicate silver chain around her neck ripple. The necklace caught my eye in the church, the charm unusual—a tiny weapon. Too long to be a regular dagger, too short to be a sword. An old-fashioned poniard.

I extend a finger and brush the toothpick-sharp tip of the blade and, with it, her skin. Her chest prickles with goosebumps, and my prize's breath hisses behind the veil.

She's not unaffected by me. Her slight reaction is a blood-bright flag unfurling before a bull. Adrenaline pounds through me, and my cock stirs. My palms itch to unwrap my gift.

I grasp the edge of the veil and lift it. My movements are slow and tender, a mockery of what a groom's should be. Once again, she surprises me. She doesn't fight me, doesn't slap my hand away. She holds still, her chest moving faster in her tight bodice.

She has the loveliest eyes, dark and velvety. She's striking rather than pretty, her jaw narrow but strong, and her nose sharp as a stiletto. Her makeup is subtle and perfect, except for those bold, blood-red lips. Not a hair of her sleek updo is out of place. For a witness to a knifing and a victim of kidnapping, she's the very picture of calm.

I want to crack her apart. I killed her groom in front of her, and she made no sound. I thought she was in shock at first, but she's remained calm.

Who is she? I researched the wedding but focused more on the layout of the church. The target was a civilian, a nobody. At first glance, his wife-to-be and guests were the same.

But this woman who wears a mini knife around her neck is more than who she seems.

I relax in my seat, letting her speak first. The car turns down an alley, weaving through the city and making its way east.

"Why?" she finally asks.

I cock my head. "Why what?"

"Why did you kill him?"

"It was a job. Nothing personal." A disappointing target, who didn't even fight back.

She snorts. "A knife to the heart? A bullet would have been easier."

My brows raise. With each passing moment, she's proving herself an enigma. Is she dangerous, like me? I hope so. Conquering her will be the sweetest challenge.

"I prefer a blade. It's more intimate. Respectful." I pat my jacket lining, where my preferred killing knife is secured.

"So you're a psychopath."

My gut kicks with an unexpected laugh. "You say it like it's a bad thing."

"I guess it's useful in your line of work."

"My line of work?"

"You're a hitman. You said it wasn't personal." She sounds impatient, as if she knows I'm being deliberately obtuse.

I was prepared for hysterics. Messy tears, blotchy skin, panicked thrashing. Even a mafia princess would lose her cool and make threats or pleas for her life.

Her controlled reactions are unexpected and so much more delicious.

"And what about you? I killed your groom in front of you."

"I'm in shock." She does not sound like she's in shock. She sounds like I interrupted her lunch.

What will she look like with her lipstick smeared from my kisses, her hair wild?

Soon I will know. My groin tightens at the thought. The monster in me roars, ready to roam free. I keep him leashed a little longer. My prey is close beside me but still wary. I want her fiery and fighting, as desperate for me as I am for her.

I've always wondered what it would be like to sample a bride on her wedding day. To touch her, feast on her, make her moan. My work offers me many depraved delights, but I've never experienced this one.

But now I have the chance. The fact that this bride might hate me only tempts me more.

I seduce her, on her wedding night, mere hours after slaughtering her betrothed.

And I will make her enjoy it.

Her veil tumbles over her brow, and she shoves it up again. I brush her hand away. Slowly, carefully, I remove each hairpin, holding her gaze.

After three pins, she looks out her window, but the red staining her olive cheeks isn't from her makeup. Finally, a reaction.

I separate the veil from her head, roll down my window, and let the wind snag the filmy white fabric. It blows away, dancing in the car's wake like a ghost. "Better?"

"Much."

I shift closer, taking up more than my fair share of the bench seat. She glares at me. I raise my chin, daring her to comment.

For a long moment, electricity crackles between us. I want to push her back onto the seat and claim her now. Only years of reining in my basest impulses allows me to deny the animal attraction that's making my heart pump faster in her presence.

Judging by the goosebumps breaking out over the mounds of her delicious breasts in the tight, white bodice, she's feeling something similar. Perhaps it's simply fear, but as someone who trades in death, terror is a useful tool. It can make a person love or hate you. Or both at the same time. Best of all, the symptoms of fear—the shortening of breath and elevated pulse—are easily confused by the body as arousal.

"What is your name?" I ask.

She presses her lips together before answering. "Vera. Yours?"

I cock my head to the side, deciding if I should tell her. "Do you really want to know?"

I let her think through the implications. Common sense says if a kidnapper lets you know his face and name, he does not intend for you to live long.

She knows this. She hesitates, and licks her lips as she thinks things through. The sight of her tongue sends a stab of arousal through my core. I shift in the seat, needing to adjust myself to relieve the pressure of my pants on my rapidly swelling cock.

"Yes," she says, and so seals her fate. My arousal is a red haze, rising like the blood lust I usually feel when I kill my quarry.

I can't stop the cruel smile twisting my lips as I tell her, "Victor."

She gives the slightest nod. Still so careful, so controlled, just like she was at the altar, where she first caught my attention. Her groom was dead, the wedding guests had fled, and she faced me silently. No screaming, no crying. No emotion. But I could sense her mind working under the veil.

If only I could slice her open, reveal her thoughts. But now is not the time for the knife. I'll have to use other weapons at my disposal to prise her apart. My words, my lips. My cock.

"You still haven't told me why you killed him."

"Your betrothed? That's between him and Stephanos. I'm just the messenger."

"Did it have to be in the middle of the wedding?"

"I was told to make it public. A spectacle. A warning not to embezzle from the Greek mob."

"Idiot," she mutters, and I know she's not talking about me. Only a fool would siphon money from Stephanos.

"Is that any way to speak of your intended?"

She bites one red lip. Makes a decision. "We weren't together that long."

That explains her lack of grief. My challenge to seduce her just became a million times easier. "Then you're welcome. For the rescue. You know what they say. . . 'Marry in haste. . .'"

She avoids my gaze, shaking her head.

"This dress doesn't suit you." I take liberties, grazing a finger over her bodice, letting it swirl over her breast. She glares like she wants to bite me.

I wish she would.

"Are you always so well armed?" I tap the necklace charm and smirk.

"Always."

I continue my exploration of her body, testing her reactions. The dress really is awful. It must have been a hand-me-down, something old, because why would she choose to wear such a thing? She would look better in armor. Something sleek and silvery. Modern.

Something worthy of the dagger at her throat.

The car reaches a stop sign and, with the barest pause, rolls through. The most important rule of leaving a crime scene is not to break any laws. I'll have to speak with Stephanos about his getaway protocol. He's not the most disciplined of leaders. It's a wonder he's hung onto his turf for so long.

"Where are we going?"

"Somewhere we can be alone." I pause, waiting for her to fight me. I set a hand on her midriff, caressing her through the stiff bodice. She stiffens, but not before I feel a tremor run through her.

The ice princess is not as frozen as she seems.

I dip my head to nuzzle her hair. Her perfume is complex, something expensive, but underneath is her pure essence. I inhale her scent, greedy for more. I tighten my grip on her, needing to rip off the confining dress. There should be nothing between me and her bare skin. My cock is a steel bar, threatening to rip my pants. Soon I will seek out her damp and secret places, to lick and suck her essence straight from the source.

The car makes its final turn. Up ahead is the bland, five-story apartment building where I make my home. I slide my palm down the curve of her breast, seeking the slight swell of her nipple under the layers of fabric.

She turns from me to stare out the window. Searching for escape? I trace a line from her nipple to the silver chain, pushing the charm aside so I can kiss the smooth line of her neck. Under my lips, her skin quivers.

As the car glides to a stop, my prize asks the question I've been waiting for. "Why did you take me?"

"Stephanos told me I could choose my reward." I touch my lips to her pulse. "I choose you."

3

Lula

I choose you, he says, like that explains it all. Does he know who I am? My last name is Romano, so he might not know my connection to the Regis family, even if he read the wedding program. He asked for my name, and I gave a fake one—Vera, my mother's name. A reminder to myself of the reason I'm here. My motivation and purpose. *My plan.*

Victor's taken me to an industrial part of town, a concrete jungle. Not a soul is on the streets, and there are barely any cars around. I get a glimpse of the driver as my captor pulls me from the car: male, with a shaved head and a full, bushy beard, his gaze fixed steadfastly forward. *Nothing to see here.* No help will come from him.

I can't run. I'll get about five steps in these shoes before Victor, the knife-loving psycho, grabs me. Better to keep playing this dangerous game.

Stephanos told me I could choose my reward. I have a hard time believing Victor would choose me as his reward, not knowing who I am. But in the backseat of the car, his interest in me had less to do with my pedigree and more to do with my body.

My treacherous body. My face still burns with the heat of my blush. *Stop it. Stop crushing on a killer.*

Victor's shadow falls over me. He smells like snow, sharp and fresh and cold. His lips are plump, but the rest of his features—cheekbones, jaw, nose—are too sharp to be human, like he's a fae king who stepped into our world and made it his winter court.

He puts a large hand at my back, and my skin tingles under my bodice. He raises a white-blond brow with an amused twist to his mouth. He's waiting to see if I'll try to run.

But... my libido gasps. *He's so pretty...*

He holds out a hand, and I almost accept it. *Stop it!*

My body keeps on betraying me as my heel twists under me, and I fall into my captor. He scoops me up in his arms and carries me, bridal style, to the front door. And like a simpering fool, I wind my arms around his neck, feeling safe and secure against him.

To anyone watching, we look like a newly married couple. Is he playing it up for any cameras? Building a case that I went with him willingly?

Probably not. When you've murdered as many people as Victor probably has, adding a kidnapping charge is no big deal.

He frees a hand for a handprint scanner to enter the building. *A keypad. Interesting.* It transforms this boring, concrete block apartment building into a villain's lair. A hitman like Victor would require nothing less.

The doors open to a sleek, square-shaped foyer, empty of anything but an elevator door and another keypad to enter it.

"Almost there, beautiful," Victor murmurs, and I blink to keep from rolling my eyes. Just because he's carrying me like a bride doesn't mean I've forgotten who he is to me. I should be fighting to get away.

Later. Victor is my best chance at getting to Stephanos. Going along with him is as good as infiltrating the Petropoulos gang. I just have to survive.

The elevator requires a third handprint before it takes us to the top floor, the doors opening directly into a dimly lit penthouse. Subtle overhead lights blink on as Victor carries me over the threshold. The air is a few degrees cooler than I expected, or maybe it's the cold, sterile nature of the decor. Most of the cavernous space is one giant room with gray concrete floors, stainless steel appliances, and white leather couches. Everything is shiny, modern, and spotless. There's a long table made from a single quartz slab, clean enough to perform surgery on. Victor could kill someone in here and easily wipe up the blood.

Maybe he already has.

"So, I'm here." My voice echoes in the massive space. "Now what?"

"You know what." His voice drops to a deeper register, and I want to roll my eyes. Except, once again, my libido is falling for it.

Since when are sexy psychopaths my type?

A strand of hair has escaped its updo, and he reaches out and winds it around his finger, rubbing his thumb over it. I resist a shiver. I am not wondering what his fingers would feel like on my naked skin. I am *not*.

"This is some Richard the Third-level fetish. Seducing a bride after you kill her groom?"

"You were having second thoughts. That is what you told me, no?" The more I talk to him, the more I detect an Eastern European accent. Not Ukrainian, but something close.

"That doesn't mean I wanted him dead."

"And yet you stood by and did nothing. No crying. No hysterics. Just rearranging your schedule in your head." Victor's glacier-blue eyes fasten on mine, intent on prising me apart.

"You make me sound so cold." And even though my exact reputation in La Famiglia is as a frigid mafia princess known for her sharp-tongued disdain, it hurts to be called callous.

"No, beautiful." He plucks at the long satin sleeve of my dress with his long fingers, and I can't hold my shiver back. "You're the opposite of cold."

My blush blooms hotter. Dammit. I can hide my thoughts but not my libido, which, after years of lying dormant, has come roaring to life. It's been a while since I've had a one-night stand. I seduced David by gazing adoringly up at him through my lashes and pretending to laugh at his bad jokes. I got him to the altar by promising to hand over my virginity (Ha!) once I was legally his.

In short, my sex life has had quite a dry spell, and now my body is ready to throw itself at this man, the blood on his hands be damned.

"Are you going to kill me?"

"I promise no harm will come to you this night."

I don't know why, but I believe him. But the lawyer in me has to close all loopholes. "And in the morning?"

He doesn't answer right away, only toys with my hair.

"Victor?" I wait, rubbing the sword charm of my necklace between a thumb and forefinger.

"We shall see."

This is the reason I believe him. He's careful about what he promises. If he's telling the truth, I have a twelve-hour window to escape.

No problem. There's a foolproof way to stay alive and send my captor to sleep.

I'm going to seduce him.

He steps closer, and the force of his presence, his striking good looks and intensity, makes me wobble.

I cast about for something to distract him. Something other than me. I'm his entertainment for the night, but I need a minute to gird my loins and get ready to perform.

"I need to use the restroom," I say, smoothing a hand over my necklace.

He steps back and waves a hand toward a room beyond the kitchen. He's got that slight smile back, the one that says he knows I'm stalling for time. That's fine. I'd rather him think I'm reluctant than guess what I'm really about.

The bathroom mirror shows a surprisingly vibrant-looking bride. There's pink in my cheeks, thanks to Victor's exploratory touches. My arousal will work to my benefit.

I just won't examine my reaction to him too closely.

There's blood on my dress. I forgot about that. Victor swung out of the way on the altar, out of the spray, but I was close enough to get spattered. The rust-colored stains already look old.

I do my business and use the sounds of the flushing toilet and running water to cover the real reason I needed a private moment. Bending over, I haul up my dress and unstrap the handgun holster hidden on my right thigh.

Are you always so well-armed?

Always.

I palm the butt of the compact weapon and let its cool weight give me strength. I strapped this gun to my leg, hoping Stephanos would come to the wedding and I could blow him away at the reception. The Sig Sauer P365 is my baby, the smallest gun I own. I'm lucky I wasn't strip-searched in the car, but my reprieve won't last long. Judging by the way Victor was looking at me, he's taking me to bed, and soon.

I could come out shooting and end the night before it begins. But then I won't get a chance to set a trap for Stephanos.

Carefully, so as not to make any telltale creaks, I open the cabinet under the sink and hide the weapon and holster behind a neat stack of toilet paper. Then I rise and wash my hands, and not a moment too soon.

The door handle turns, and Victor saunters in. I didn't lock the door on purpose—in case the clicking sound alerted him to the fact that I had something to hide. I expected him to respect my need for privacy.

My reprieve is over.

I meet his gaze in the mirror. My cheeks flush even further. With my red lips, I look more than ready to play seductress. "Help me with my dress?"

He steps forward, crowding me. I lean over the bathroom counter until the sword on my necklace points into the sink and stare at Victor in the mirror. His favorite knife makes its appearance, flashing between us. Every muscle in me goes rigid.

Victor slides the knife up the back of my dress, slicing off the old-fashioned buttons. The dress sags, the puffed sleeves wilting off my shoulders. I go to strip them off, but Victor tsks, "No," and waves the knife, his icy eyes holding mine in the mirror. "Do not move." He sets the blade at my back against my skin. Close enough to shave the soft hairs there. "Do not even breathe." He slices the rest of the bindings away.

The weight of the fabric makes the dress fall with a heavy, rustling sound, leaving me naked but for my sheer stockings, garter belt, bra, and panties.

I had a plan for my wedding night. A few bottles of wine and a bit of Rohypnol in David's glass, and I could spill a little blood on the sheets and coo to him in the morning that he was amazing. Idiot that he was, he'd believe it. He believed when I said I loved him, that I was a virgin, and that I'd give myself fully to him as soon as we were married.

For my own pleasure, I wore my favorite set of sheer lingerie in a bright, cheerful color. *Something blue.* The exact color of Victor's eyes.

I don't believe in fate, not like my cousin Royal. But if I did, I'd say she's up to something. The bitch.

In his dark suit, Victor makes a somber frame for my naked self. The black of his pupils has grown to swallow up the blue. He murmurs something in his native tongue. A curse or a compliment, something low and soothing to steady me as he traces his long fingers over my back and shoulders, down my arms. It'd be more relaxing if he wasn't still holding the knife.

I swallow and dig for my courage. Before I can turn, he presses into my back, pinning my hips against the sink. I can't stop the flare of fear in my eyes. He glides his hand over the flat of my stomach, the handle of his knife imprinting my skin. "So beautiful," he murmurs into the curve of my shoulder, kissing the tender junction at the base of my neck.

It'd be so easy for him to bring up the knife and hold it

to my throat, looking deep into my eyes and slicing my jugular while murmuring sweet nothings into my ears. He could so easily do it, but something tells me he won't. I don't know why I'm so sure. I lean into my captor's strong embrace, letting my breasts rise and fall in time to my rapid heartbeat. I didn't take the time to kick off my heels, and with their added inches, I'm tall enough that his cock probes my backside.

Then he kicks my legs apart. I watch Death's beautiful face, helpless to stop him as he slips his left hand between my legs. His eyes widen when he discovers my secret, the one I've been keeping from him.

I'm so fucking wet, wetter than I've ever been before. Does the threat of being stabbed turn me on? Is the fear an aphrodisiac, making me crave the basest proof that I'm alive?

He holds me between his hands, his right hand on my belly, the knife an unspoken threat, his left stroking over the soaked gusset of my La Perla panties in a come-hither motion. Arousal flares deep in my belly. I hold out for several long minutes, but when his middle finger presses through the fabric to tease my sensitive opening, my eyes flutter and almost close.

"Look at me," he orders, and I obey, grateful for the harsh rasp of his voice. Better to not lose myself. Better to not take my eyes off my adversary.

He dips his head, breathes in deeply, and drops a kiss on my shoulder. He brings the knife up and across my collarbone to my bra strap and, with a small *snick*, bares my left breast. Goosebumps rise all over my chest, and he rubs at them, finding my nipple and thumbing it. I swallow my breath and hold still. The knife blade is *right there.* And he knows I'm aware of it, that I'm afraid. With a cruel twist to his lips, he flips the blade in midair and palms the sharp edge to use the handle as a second digit, pinching my nipple between it and his thumb.

It's too much. I cum in a rush, shaking silently. Heat and a pink stain flood my chest. I stifle my cries but can't hide my reaction from him.

I just came in my captor's arms.

He releases my nipple and flips the knife again to use the blade to slice away my panties. The rest of my bra is next. He spares the garter belt and stockings, but they only emphasize how naked and vulnerable I am before him.

He raises his left hand, the one that made me cum. My pussy soaked his cuff. He licks my essence off his fingers, watching my face in the mirror.

Once more, he palms the sharp edge of the knife before lowering it between my legs. He presses the handle into me. The base of the knife slides in smoothly, my juices easing the way.

I jerk in his arms, and he clamps his free arm around me, holding me between him and the sink. We make a pretty picture—a naked woman, her chest flushed from orgasm, and a beautiful man behind her, securing her against his powerful, suit-clad frame. You just have to look closely to see the tip of a knife in his hand and the monster lurking in the corner of his smile.

He slides the knife handle in and out of me, fucking me so deep I feel it behind my belly button. He knows just how to angle the weapon, how to drag it across the sweet spots inside me. I shudder, fighting my rising orgasm.

"Don't resist, beautiful," he breathes, drawing the handle out and pushing it back in. My soaked pussy makes a squelching sound. "Surrender."

A series of thrusts with the knife handle trigger my G-spot, and it's all over. I come again, this time with a low, breathless rush of air, not quite a moan.

"So quiet." Victor laughs softly in my ear. "So controlled. I'm going to make you scream for me."

He tips me forward and braces his left hand on my hip. Teetering off balance, I slap a hand against the mirror to hold me upright and look into my own dark eyes. My cheeks are flushed red. My captor made me come, not once, but twice.

And he's not done.

Victor plants his right hand on the mirror next to mine. He's still holding the knife, the handle slick and shiny with my cum, and the long blade clinks against the glass.

My gun's right under the sink. It'd take me a moment to grab it, but I could distract him and do it at any time. But he promised I'd survive tonight.

His breathing is harsh, puffing against my hair. He tugs at his clothes with his free hand, baring only the essential part of him to plunge into me. A hitch, an adjustment, and he presses his hand over mine, pinning me with his body and his gaze. The head of his cock nudges my entrance, and my pussy weeps with need. With one long thrust, he stabs his cock into me, driving me to my tiptoes. I bow over the counter, my necklace clinking on the marble, my cries echoing in the small space. I lose contact with the floor and one heel, then the other drops to the floor. Victor wraps his arm around my midriff, propping me higher. I'm taller than the average woman and no lightweight, but I feel like a rag doll, plucked off the ground, dangling in from his hold. A toy in his hands. Victor drives into me, and I take it all, my mouth open and red lips rounded. He strokes into me, a merciless pounding beat.

And I cum, bouncing and quivering on his rod. A pin in

my updo comes loose, and my dark hair tumbles down, veiling my face. I toss my head back and forth, trying to shake the strands of hair away from my eyes. The sword dances under my throat.

"Yes," Victor growls and I realize I'm whimpering *No, no, no*. My arousal is rising again, an inexorable wave of pleasure threatening to tow me under. My pussy clenches on his dick, trying to suck him in deeper.

I slap the mirror again and again, fighting to gain purchase and angle my hips to take more of Victor's giant dick. It's swollen further inside me, knocking at my cervix and so deep I go cross-eyed. Heat blooms in my head and core, and I'm cumming again, the spasms sending Victor over the edge. He pushes me up until my body drapes over the counter, and my cheek is plastered against the mirror. I focus on the knife blade shining inches from my face.

And then it's over, and he's cumming, his cock pulsing inside me hard enough to set off another round of mini orgasms inside me. I slump down, too wrung out to prop myself up.

He gathers me into his arms, stroking the hair out of my eyes. For a moment, he cups my cheek with his big hand.

Then he pushes me to my knees. I sink onto the thick Persian rug that covers the tile, narrowly avoiding kneeling on my fallen heels. Victor's cock bobs in front of my face, shockingly dark compared to the paleness of the rest of him, huge and hard and slick with my own essence. I open my mouth, but he steps back and sets the knife handle at my lips.

"Lick," he orders, gathering my hair in his hands. Arousal surges through me, thundering in my ears, and I lean forward and extend my tongue. I lick up the smooth handle, tasting myself. When he pushes, forcing my head back, I relax my throat and allow him to penetrate me with his knife all the way to the heel.

My eyes flare with slight panic, and his own hooded ones grow heavy in response. *Sadist.* I ignore the needy throb in my already well-used pussy and dig my fingers into the folds of his pant legs, my senses swimming with him. He's fucking my mouth with the knife he used to kill David only hours ago. And I'm doing my best to choke it down.

Finally, he releases me, sliding the knife out of my mouth. He swipes a thumb across my lower lip, and I remember I'm wearing my favorite color lipstick. Dark red, the color of spilled blood. Too bold for regular use and too bold for a bride. My own tiny act of defiance.

Victor murmurs something in his native tongue, soft and crooning like a lullaby. "Good girl." He slides a hand up my cheek, and I fight not to press into it, to accept his approval. I need to remember what I'm doing here.

Seduce him. Survive.

Never surrender.

His cock is inches away from my face. Makes my insides cramp just thinking about it invading me. I'm glad I'm on birth control.

If I plan to seduce him, I better start now. I reach for his cock, and he tugs me back by my hair. "No. Not here. I'm not through with you."

He hauls me up by my arms and tosses me over his shoulder. My dark hair tumbles over my face, my eyes flashing to my wary reflection before he flips the light and carries me from the room.

4

V*ictor*

My prize doesn't struggle as I carry her to where I want her. My bedroom. I lay her on the bed and fix her with a pointed finger. "Stay."

She glares at me, and I pause, waiting for her rebellion with my head tilted to the side. "Unless you want me to tie you to the bed?"

She looks like she might argue but stops when I raise a hand to undo my cufflinks and toss them on a dresser. I start on my jacket and dress shirt buttons, and she leans back, drinking in each new inch of my exposed chest. I turn my head to hide a grin. I thought she might like a show.

I fucked her without undressing, too impatient to be balls deep in her. There's something about her that brings out the beast in me. I've never been so swollen with need, so out of control.

There's no need to rush. She is mine as long as I wish it. I've never wanted a woman past one night, but if that's not long enough to quench my desire for her, then there's no reason I can't keep her longer. Indefinitely.

Forever.

I blink away the fantasy of her lying in my bed, hair unfurled on the pillow, blinking in the morning light. I don't need to imagine her when she's right here, naked on my bed, laid out like a sacrifice.

"Spread your legs," I command, propping a foot on the stool at the base of my bed to untie my shoes. "Show me that pretty pussy."

She deliberates with her chin tipped down. I remove my shoes and socks before it's clear she's not going to obey.

Excellent.

"What, shy?" I drawl. "You came hard enough on my knife not so long ago. And again on my cock."

Her nostrils flare as she visibly bites back a response. I make quick work of the rest of my clothes and stalk to the bed. My shadow falls over her, but she doesn't flinch. She raises her chin to challenge me, and I grip it in my palm. Her eyes are dark with desire. "Are you going to fight me?"

Her tongue touches her upper lip. "No." Her voice is heavy, husky. "No, I want this."

"If you want this," I grip my cock with my free hand, an obscene gesture that makes it clear what we're talking about, "then you obey."

With her jaw in my grasp, she can't shake her head. But she does roll her eyes. I tighten my grip on her face. "No?"

She presses up to her knees. Even on the bed, she can't match my height, but she doesn't back down. "You don't want that."

I slide my hand from her jaw to her throat. If she gets the threat, she doesn't acknowledge it. She presses her hands to my bare skin. A shock runs through me at her touch, my body trembling like a racehorse ready to run. She smirks like she knows her control over me.

"Obeying is the quickest way for you to be bored with me. And if you're bored, I die."

"You think so?"

She slides a hand south and replaces my fingers on my cock with her own. "I know so."

"You don't seem afraid." I release her neck to trace her lips. The corner of her mouth curls under my finger.

"Maybe I like a challenge too." She squeezes my cock, and I groan deep in my throat. I have to fight not to thrust into her palm. Naked but for a garter belt and stockings, on her knees, she's found the upper hand.

Not for long. I grip her hair and draw her back until she's lying on the bed. She loses her grip on my dick, and I loom over her. "Nice try."

I ease her knees apart and let my hand fall, smacking her dead on her pussy. She throws her head back, her neck working on a silent cry. "That's for not following instructions."

Her chest heaves, but she doesn't let a sound slip. I slide two fingers up and down her folds. She's soaking wet, filled with my cum. She can hide many things from me, but her pussy does not lie.

Her reactions leave me wanting. Her breath trembles, but no cry or moan escapes.

I stroke her slick flesh, studying her solemn face. "Who taught you to be so quiet?"

She shakes her head slightly and doesn't answer.

"This will not do." With my free hand, I massage her scalp until her eyelids droop. "I want to hear you. Your cries and sobs, everything in between." Her lips part, her breath growing languid. "Can you do that for me?"

"I've never done it before," she whispers.

"So tense." I've half-folded her in my arms. It'd be an innocent pose if I didn't have my fingers circling her clit. "So in control. What would it be like to give yourself to me?"

Her eyes flick open. "So you can knife me in my sleep?"

"My knife is over there." I nod to my dresser. "If I wanted to kill you, I'd have done it before now."

She barks out a laugh and relaxes more. "I guess you're right." She leans back. The sword on her necklace is askew, poking into her collarbone, and she straightens it before stretching her arms overhead. Her back arches, pushing her breasts up on display. "How do you want me?"

"Like this." With her draped backward, I can play with her pussy as long as I want. "But let go, beautiful." I paint her red lips with her own juices and reposition myself between her legs. "And scream for me."

Lula

Victor lowers his blond head between my knees. I clench up automatically, but the giant hitman is surprisingly gentle. He strokes his fingers up and down my sex, delving into the folds. He finds my clit and circles it, forcing my already wrung-out body to stir. My arousal lifts its head.

He's right. He's unarmed, his knife out of reach. But his body is lethal all on its own. In the dappled shadows untouched by the low light, his large frame is impossibly beautiful. His torso is a work of art, each muscle sleek and refined. I crane my head and get a glimpse of his perfect ass right as he swipes his tongue up my center.

"Oooooh." The barest moan slips out of me.

He chuckles straight into my pussy. "That's it, my beauty. Let me know what you like."

For a heartless assassin, he's pretty considerate. But there's nothing polite about the way he presses his face into me, tongue fucking my entrance. My hips rock of their own volition, riding him. The breadth of his powerful shoulders is the only thing stopping me from squeezing his head in a vise grip with my thighs.

Is this the time to make my move? My gun is rooms away, and he can still overpower me.

Victor angles his head, nibbling the inside of my thigh while his fingers twist inside me. I'm so fucking wet.

He reaches up and squeezes my breast. "You're thinking too much." He rises over me, a dark god in his natural lair. The light gilds his hair. "And you need to pay attention." He rubs the inner wall of my pussy, massaging my G-spot and tugging my orgasm closer. "To me. And only me." He dips down to cover my breast with his mouth. The heat makes me melt into the bed. I want to fight it, to push him away, but his fingers and mouth are magic, turning the world hazy. I couldn't fight him if I tried.

His teeth find my nipple, and I gasp at the slight pinch. My pussy clamps down on his fingers.

"So it's a touch of pain that does it," Victor muses, his mouth still between my breasts. "I wonder. . ." His fingers turn cruel, pinching my flesh, his thumb at my clit, and the rest of his fingers stretching my entrance. It's almost too much, and I'm gasping, my mouth open as if that will allow my pussy to widen and accept him.

He bites my nipple again, scraping the tender bud, and it's too much. The points of pain at my breast and core light up, the sensation combining and cascading through me. White heat fills me, shocking every nerve ending. I cum, jerking hard enough to levitate off the bed. Victor pins me, crooning praise and pressing kisses to my breasts.

I come down slowly, my ears ringing from my cries. My groin aches from the constant onslaught of orgasms.

"Very good. So beautiful." Two of his fingers are still inside of me, but he's eased the pressure of his thumb. He's got the whole of me in the palm of his hand.

"My god," I croak. "I've come more tonight with you than with all of my other lovers... combined."

"That says less about me than it does about them."

My laugh blooms bright in the dark. "You're right. Oh god." His shadow falls over me, and I cover my face with my hands. "I slept with my fiancé's killer."

"And enjoyed it. A better wedding night than you expected?"

Yes. I clamp my lips shut. If he wants me to admit that, he'll have to wait a long time.

He takes my silence as a challenge and tugs me closer by my legs, angling his hips and guiding his cock to glide deep into me. He props my legs over his shoulders, and I'm grateful for my religious yoga practice as he leans over me, bending me in half. My body is his plaything, a doll, a toy to prop the way he wants. I can claim to hate it, but as the head of his cock stretches my entrance, I can't deny the heat of arousal flooding me. I want his weight on me, the muscles heavy and honed to perfection. I want his hands on me, his fingers cruel and clever from their deadly work.

I want him. I can lie to him, but I can't lie to myself. The brutal burn of shame only makes the pleasure more exquisite.

I shout to the ceiling as he plunges into me, filling me to the brim and sending me spiraling higher and higher. My body snaps and sizzles like an exposed wire, and my cries echo on and on into the night.

5

Lula

I WAKE SLOWLY, the taste of cotton in my mouth and a heavy soreness in my limbs. I raise my head, blinking in the hazy gray light, and the slight movement sends twinges through my core, reminding me of the hours I spent impaled on Victor's monster dick.

All night. He fucked me with a knife handle. And then he just plain fucked me.

Scream for me, he ordered, and I did. My throat is raw from crying out. He ate me out and fucked me over and over again. And I orgasmed.

A lot.

And I want to do it again.

Victor lies beside me, tangled in the sheets. His broad body looks no less powerful now that it's at rest, but his face is peaceful. The boyish, white-blond hair is at odds with the sculpted perfection of his face. He's lovely, too lovely for words, an angel fallen to earth.

I've seen him hunt his quarry, a killer intent on his prey. I've seen him amused and arrogant, smirking as he alternately taunts me or commands me to obey. It was easy to hate him then. But watching him sleep, his large form denting the bed and his pale eyelashes fanned out on his cheeks, tender feelings stir inside me. What would it be like to wake up to someone like this, morning after morning, day after day?

It's a crazy thought. I need to harden myself. To be ready to do what I must. Victor is a pawn in this game of vengeance. A means to an end. Our time is finished.

There's no use dreaming of what might have been.

I rise silently and pad to the bathroom to do my business. The shreds of my wedding dress lie in piles on the floor. I'll have to borrow clothes.

I touch my chest and realize my necklace is gone. Fallen off or ripped from me in the throes of passion, but I don't have time to search for it.

I slip on the white satin heels—the only item of clothing to survive the night—and crouch to pull out my gun.

Forget Victor. I'm closer to Stephanos than I've ever been. Time to set the trap and close in for the kill.

Victor

I WAKE with a sense of languid peace and the taste of defiled bride in my mouth. My eyes and body feel heavy, like I slept solid and haven't moved for hours. I haven't had a full night's sleep in a long, long time. Maybe not since I was a baby.

The bride—Vera—banished my bad dreams.

She's awake now, moving around in the apartment. Trying to escape? As much as I wanted to wake up with a beautiful naked woman stretched out beside me, I wanted to know what she would do if I left her to her own ends.

I didn't expect to sleep so deeply. Perhaps I should have tied her up before succumbing to slumber.

Perhaps I will tonight. I've never wanted more than one night with a woman, but this one is different. She contains a puzzle I have yet to solve.

Something stabs my palm, and I open it, unsurprised to see the tiny dagger poking the muscle under my thumb. I turn it so it bisects my palm from top to bottom. I tore her necklace off while I rode her and gripped it all night while I slept.

Soft steps sound in the hallway, and I relax into the bed. She didn't leave. I wonder at the sense of relief rushing through me. Another puzzle for me to piece together.

The door swings open, and I raise my head, ready to greet her with a smile.

The first thing to enter is the tiny barrel of a gray pistol. It's small, delicate, and suited to Vera's fine-boned hand. Vera appears next in an intriguing new outfit—my tan trench coat and her heels. Is she naked underneath? The sight of her inspires a whole new round of fantasies.

She's pointing the weapon straight at my chest.

So this is what she was hiding under all that white satin. I was too obsessed with my win, too assured of my victory, to pat her down.

Are you always so well-armed?

The dagger in my fist bites my skin. I tighten my grip, unwilling to show her what I'm holding and start to sit up.

"No," she barks, steadying the gun. "Stay there."

"What is this?"

"You had your fun; now it's my turn."

I settle back on the pillows, smirking. "You had fun too, beautiful."

She ignores this, though the faint color cresting her cheeks tells me she's not as unaffected as she wants to be. "Don't move. Don't even breathe." She reaches into the pocket of my coat and holds up a small black cell. "What's the code?"

It's the burner I've been using for this contract. I was planning on dumping it today after contacting Stephanos to ensure I received the last payment.

"You're full of surprises." I give her the code. She taps it in without looking.

I could rush and tackle her. I might catch a bullet, or I might not. She hasn't proven whether she can even shoot.

But then I'll never know what happens next.

We stare at each other, the pistol between us.

She didn't kill me in my sleep or when I forced her into the car. She didn't try to stop her groom's death, either. Last night, she let me strip her down and fuck her to orgasm. Over and over.

"If you're unhappy with my lovemaking, there's no need to shoot me." I relax back on the bed. "Come and let me make it up to you."

"Shut up." There's no flicker of emotion on her face. I can't see the wheels of deliberation turning inside her mind, but I know she's trying to figure out what to do with me.

What is her endgame? No matter how things unfold, it's

clear: Vera's the most interesting thing that's happened to me in years.

"There are handcuffs in the side drawer—" I meant to give her an option, but she interrupts.

"Were you going to kill me?"

"Not last night. Not today. Not as long as you proved interesting."

"Thank you for your honesty." She nods. She's come to a decision. "It's nothing personal."

Something bites me in the gut a second before my ears register the crack of a gunshot.

Lula

By the time I make it to Three Diner, I'm limping in my high heels. Walking ten blocks from Victor's building was enough to give me blisters.

I replayed shooting Victor the whole time. His pained grunt was the only sound to escape his gritted teeth, but his eyes drove needles of ice my way. I didn't stay and wait for the blood to well up from the wound in his naked chest, but in my mind's eye, the movie plays on. The rich, wine-colored stain spreads on the white sheets to the soundtrack of the big man's labored breathing.

Victor is the first person I've shot, but he won't be the last. He was a pit stop on my road to vengeance, and I'm done with him. There's no turning back.

I'll just have to ignore the way my body aches from the orgasms he gave me.

My destination is a long, low building on the edge of

Unitatem University. It looks like a trailer and an Airstream had a baby, and the result is this silver-sided diner. The pink neon "3" sign has marked its spot for over fifty years.

I slap my palm on the door frame and walk in, Victor's trench coat fluttering around my stocking-clad calves. I'm bare-assed underneath, like a call girl catering to her client's specific fantasy. Only my stockings, shoes, and garter belt survived Victor's blade, and this morning, I didn't spend any time rifling through Victor's drawers for clothes. I grabbed a coat and his burner phone, shot him, and left.

My aim is good—years of going to the range with my father's men ensured that. I could've targeted the T-zone, the spot between the eyebrows. A bullet there means instant death. Clean and quick. Too good for a cold-blooded murderer like Victor.

But something stayed my hand.

I shot him in the stomach. Gut wounds lead to a slow and painful death. But if he can drag himself to a phone and get to a doctor in time... I'd put his survival rate at fifty/fifty.

I refuse to feel guilty. Victor would feel no regret about cutting me down. There's no reason I should spare him a second thought. I only knew him for one night.

But... oh, what a night.

The diner is dark inside, with most of the light coming from the freezer chest to my right, illuminating racks and racks of fluffy-topped lemon meringue pies. The diner decor is straight out of the 1950s because that's the last time this place was renovated. Faded red leather booths and metal tables line the window side. A long bar with red-topped metal stools line the other. The walls are painted teal and surprisingly clean. The air is pure *eau de pomme frites.* If they could bottle it into a perfume, I'd wear it every day.

"Party of one?" The waitress grabs a plastic menu

without looking at me. The servers here are notoriously rude, but no customer would dare say anything about it. "Booth or bar?" She's got the rasp of a seventy-year-old smoker, and her pink and white short-sleeved uniform shows off the dark tattoos whorling up both arms.

"Booth, please." Just because the service here is rude doesn't mean I get to be.

The waitress hustles away without checking to make sure that I follow. I clip-clop after her in my stupid heels. The place is empty save for an old timer at the bar who hasn't left his spot in four decades and two workmen in a nearby booth. The two men glance up at me as I pass and instantly look away. I must have my ice-princess face back on. Either that, or they know not to look at customers of Three Diner too closely.

"Coffee?" the waitress asks, slapping the menu in front of me.

"Please. And the special, when you get a chance. Number three."

Her fake lashes don't flicker as I give the code. She nods at the menu and walks off.

I drum my nails on the metal table top. The scent of scrambled eggs and homestyle fries makes my mouth water, but if I eat now, I'll fall asleep. I check the lapels of Victor's coat to make sure it hasn't gaped open to give those workmen a peep show.

Three Diner has three owners. I don't know who I'll get today. The eldest, the younger sister, or the daughter they adopted together.

In less than five minutes, a young, redheaded woman in dark glasses glides into the booth opposite me. She's pale and tall, her arms too thin in the pink and white uniform.

The waitress swings by to serve us both cups of coffee, and the young woman waits until she leaves to speak.

"Lucrezia Romano," she says in a melodious tone. Her hair clashes with the pink in her uniform but frames her face perfectly. She's startlingly lovely, but none of the workmen give her so much as a glance. Not that she noticed them. She's blind under those dark, round John Lennon glasses.

"You asked for the special?" Her voice rings like a bell across a city square.

"I did," I confirm.

"How can we help you?"

"I have an appointment today at noon. With Stephanos."

Her lips pinch together. "My mothers told me you've been here before asking for his location."

"Now I have it." I set the burner phone Victor unlocked for me on the table. I impersonated Victor enough to get Stephanos to send over the meeting place, a restaurant on the edge of his territory. "I pay the tithe."

"You have for some time, or so my mothers tell me. You've been on this quest for so long." Her voice echoes strangely, as if we're in a grand cathedral and not a cramped diner. "I will give you the choice now to turn back."

I lean in. "There is no turning back. I know Stephanos murdered my mother. It's taken me years to uncover this information, and by the time I did, my father was too old to do anything about it."

"And your brother?"

I don't ask how she knows about Gino. I just scoff.

She nods. "Your quest is true. We will aid you, but we require a boon." She slides the burner phone back towards me. "Speak to your cousin. He knows you're a frequent patron of ours. He's been calling for you. Use the phone booth in the corner."

I head to the phone booth and settle in. As soon as I sit down, the phone in front of me rings with a bright sound. I wince and pick it up.

"Lula." Royal uses my family nickname. "Where are you?"

"You know where I am. I'm surprised you don't have eyes on this place."

"I heard about the wedding. You didn't invite me?"

"I knew you wouldn't approve."

He curses in Italian, softly enough that I know his wife Leah must be just out of earshot. "This is madness," he says. "What can I say or do to turn you back?"

"There's nothing," my voice chokes up. "Tell my brother that it's over."

"I could kill your father for putting you on this crazy quest."

"He's already dead." And so am I. Royal and I both know there's little chance I'll come back from this. I'm going to walk into Stephanos' lair with all the weapons I can carry.

"At least tell me your plan. I can send backup. I will support you in this."

"No, you can't. You don't have enough men." Our family is still reeling from the stupid moves his father made. "And we still don't know who the mole is." While he was in charge, Royal's father had gone so far as to make deals with Stephanos. We did our best to sever the relationship, but now and again, shipments would go missing.

"Whoever it is will run to Stephanos and warn him as soon as you give the word about our plan."

Royal curses.

I'm right, and he knows it.

"Lula, per l'amor di Dio—"

Instead of hanging up, I place the phone down, letting Royal continue to try to convince the empty booth not to walk into the lion's den alone.

Royal will never forgive me for what I'm about to do. But it won't matter because I'll be dead.

Something clicks, and a secret panel opens in front of my legs, offering a black briefcase. I lean down and take it. It's heavier than it looks, but I steel my arm and carry it out of the phone booth.

The redhead is waiting. "Follow me." She leads me back through the kitchen, past two stocky, short-order cooks with tattoo sleeves. The scent of French fries and fried meat is strongest here, and the air has an oily thickness to it that makes it feel like grease is coating my skin.

Near the back door, a white-haired woman with a red bandana wrapped around her head sits hunched over a big silver bowl, peeling potatoes. A mountain of brown peels is piled next to her. My guide stops in front of her. We both wait in respectful silence for the old woman to raise her head.

"Madonna," I murmur.

"Oh no, not me," the old woman cackles and nods to the far side of the kitchen, where a tall woman stands, Viking-blonde hair with threads of gray streaking through it pulled back, stirring a large pot of soup. "That would be that one. And I see you've met our young one. I'm the other."

"It is an honor." I bow my head.

The old woman narrows her eyes. "I knew your mother. Her name was Vera, was it not?"

"Yes."

"You seek the truth, and you seek her. May you find both in the end." She pats my cheek with a clawed hand.

The young red-headed woman leads me out the back door, where a discreet black car is waiting. A burly man in dark glasses sits in the driver's seat.

"He will drop you off," she tells me, the dark glasses turned to my face. I imagine her blind eyes underneath, big and wide and unblinking as an owl's.

"Thank you," I say.

"Consider services rendered," she intones in that high-priestess voice. "Your tithe will be terminated at the end of the day."

I don't bother to tell her there's no point, that I've left a significant portion of my will to the diner and the three women who run it.

My mother was the one who first took me to Three Diner when I was little. I sat in the booth and swung my legs, too short to reach the floor. I drank a milkshake as my mother spoke in whispers, first to the tattooed waitress and then to the Viking-blonde woman who came out of the back with the scent of fry oil. She never told me why we were there. To this day, I don't know. But I'll never forget what she told me.

"The diner is a place for women who need help."

It gives me hope to know the diner will be there for women in need long after I am gone.

Once I'm safe in the backseat of the car, I give the driver the address of our destination. The car glides a few feet and turns onto the main road. As the diner's dark neon sign disappears in the rearview mirror, I balance the briefcase on my legs and open it.

The weapons are packed in the foam like jewels, black and sleek and deadly. A fully loaded Sig 320 with a suppressor underneath. Extra bullets for my P365. A holster for both. And a small silver tube that turns out to be lipstick in my favorite dark red shade.

By the time we reach the rundown restaurant where Stephanos holds court, I'm fully armed, the Sig 320 deep in the pocket of the trench coat, my P365 strapped to my thigh, and a fresh coat of war paint on my lips.

"Cut through here," I order, and the driver obeys, taking a sharp turn down an alley that's barely an inch wider than our car. I hold my breath as if that will help us squeeze through. We reach the street, and he stops the car.

"Fates be with you," he says.

I slide out of the car, tightening the belt of Victor's coat so it's secure around me, and march past the dumpsters to the restaurant where Stephanos waits. As I get closer, I slow my steps, letting my hips roll suggestively under my coat. The chilly air licks up my bare legs as I find a side door and slip inside.

Inside, dust motes dance in the air. The restaurant is dim and filled with faded decor and the stench of stale cigarettes. There are stains on the carpet that make me shudder to think of the state of the kitchens. The cooks and workers are too busy banging pots and pans and cursing to notice me. I float to the front and into the heart of the restaurant, past stacked chairs and an empty hostess stand.

The place isn't open yet and probably doesn't do much business besides host Stephanos' business meetings and launder his money. He has a bunch of these places in his territory and moves between them constantly. His paranoia keeps him alive. It certainly kept me from tracking him down sooner and putting a bullet between his eyes.

There's a light on in the back of the restaurant, and the sound of muttered voices filters out as I approach it. Two big men with unshaven chins stand guard outside a back room.

They turn in unison and still as they clock me. Twin cigarettes flare in the shadows.

"Can I help yous, sweetheart?"

"I'm here about a birthday surprise?" I keep my voice low and purring, with a slight Jersey Shore accent. I pose, putting my weight on my left leg, the one with my small Sig Sauer strapped to my thigh, and let my right one peek out of the coat, flashing my knee and garter strap. Both men's eyes snap down. I toss back my hair and part the top of the coat enough to give them a glimpse of the swell of my breasts without compromising the tight belt around my waist. I lick my lips and flutter my lashes.

Sexy call girl, that's me.

"C'mere." One of the men crooks his finger, and I sway towards him.

If he pats me down, I'll have to shoot him in the gut and make a run for it. I let his eyes crawl over me for one long minute.

He just pats my bottom. "Have fun in there." He smirks.

I let my lips curve up. "Maybe I'll find you when I'm done." I wink and sashay past him, down the hall towards the room towards the murmur of male voices. My heartbeat booms in my ears.

There's an emergency exit at the end of the hall. I could glide down and escape through it, walk a few blocks away, and call Royal for backup. He'd come and help me, and in the end, he'd take me home.

Instead, I take a deep breath and turn into the larger room. It's a room within a room, with booths lining four low walls to form a smaller square with a dark corridor around the perimeter for waitresses to scurry back and forth. At the back wall, a group of men sit along one long table. Cigar smoke hangs heavy in the air, even though it's still morning.

"He's late. The fuck," someone, probably Stephanos, is muttering. "Bruno, go call him."

A giant with a shaved head—Bruno—rises obediently. A minute earlier, Bruno would be sitting, blinking sleepily into his tiny white espresso cup. A few minutes later, he'd be out of the room, and I'd have had a clear shot.

Instead, his big, shaven head snaps up, eyes fastening on me. Instead of a call girl, he sees what I actually am: a threat. Years of instinct kick in. "Oi!" he shouts.

I let my coat fall open, and for a blissful second, every man's eyes freeze on my naked breasts long enough for me to draw the gun in my pocket and crack off a shot.

I aim for the man who gave Bruno the order. The only clear photos of my nemesis are from a few years ago. But this has to be Stephanos, mean-eyed, squat, and ugly, with a few thin gray hairs clinging to his balding scalp.

My first shot clips his shoulder. He bellows, and I'm already aiming for his heart. But it doesn't matter because Bruno flips the table.

Cups and saucers go flying, men bellow, and wood splinters around me. I duck into one of the booths and return fire.

Bullets whizz around me. The two men who were supposed to be guarding the door run in, guns drawn to eliminate the threat, and get mowed down in the crossfire. One does a grisly dance in front of me, blasted on both sides by my Sig and friendly fire.

Bodies slump between us. More men are running, fleeing to save their own skin. It doesn't matter.

Somewhere behind the shield of a heavy restaurant table, Stephanos is on the floor, groaning. This is my chance to end him, and it's slipping away from me.

I grab a chair to cover me and dart to a closer booth.

Bruno rises, howling, with a gun in either hand. I cringe away from the double barrels. He fires, and I dive behind one of the low walls. Something bites my thigh. Pain blasts up my leg and recedes to nothing, numbed by adrenaline.

Smoke fills the dingy restaurant. The gunfire cracks, so close and loud I might as well be deaf.

Through the screen of gray air and muffled sounds, I return fire until the Sig is out. I should've asked the diner ladies for an assault rifle. Ears ringing, I grab my backup out of its holster, but in the time it takes to do so, Bruno grabs his boss and drags him off the floor. They're gone, disappearing behind the opposite wall. I could chase them all the way to the front of the restaurant, but Bruno will take his last stand there, and I'll probably have to shoot my way through his rallied troops while Stephanos jumps into a getaway car and makes his cowardly escape.

The smoke is clearing. The floor is littered with black mounds of dead mobsters in dark suits. One of them gurgles, and the stench of blood and shit stains the air.

I rise and dash past the far wall. No one shoots. No one stops me. But I'm sobbing as I hit the emergency door and emerge into the bright day, trying not to think of how, for the second time in twenty-four hours, my plan for vengeance is bleeding out on the floor.

6

L*ula*

Three months later...

As far as safe houses go, a three-story house on the river isn't bad. Here, I do my work on a secure server, mostly contracts for businesses or land deals that Royal makes with one of the other families that rule Metropolis. Rebuilding what our idiot fathers gambled away.

An hour after my shootout with Bruno, Royal picked me up and brought me to his home. He sent men to the restaurant, but the place was cleared out, with only a few bodies left on the floor. We had a shouting fight that he won, and then he brought me straight here under the cover of night.

Rumor on the street is that Stephanos is still alive, suffering minor injuries from a bullet to the shoulder. He's convalescing the same way he's survived the past few decades, by burrowing deep into Metropolis' underworld like a rat. He's spent a lifetime avoiding the four main crime Families, carving out a living on the edges of our territory, scavenging for scraps, and he's good at it.

My mother's death is still unavenged. But I'm alive and hidden from retaliation in a safe house Royal insisted on. I have a desk and a row machine on the deck facing the water. It's boring in a Zen way.

Today, the heat is a heavy blanket in the air, making the afternoon hours stretch long and lazy. It's perfect for naps but less perfect for trying to focus on contract law. Alas, contract law is what pays the bills.

My phone rings, and I reach for it, only to realize it's not my cell. It's another phone I keep tucked away like a dirty secret—the burner I took from Victor after our night together. I don't know why I held on to it, much less kept it charged and close by. It sits in its own bottom drawer, and now it's buzzing angrily, waiting for me to make a decision. I snatch it up and answer it, but keep quiet as I hold it to my ear.

The moment is charged with electricity. There's a twinge in my thigh right where I was wounded in the shootout.

There's silence on the other end of the line. I bite my lip to keep from shrieking. Who is this? Who called me? As far as I know, only Victor used this phone and only to contact Stephanos. It's standard protocol for a professional hitman —buy a burner phone, use it for a single job, then toss it. I never tried using the phone to lock onto Stephanos. I didn't think it would work. Could he be calling now?

I'm about to say something when I hear a slight sound. A sigh, a heavy gust of labored breathing, and then one word.

"Vera."

I hang up and let the burner phone fall into its drawer with a clatter. Adrenaline blasts up my arms, screaming at me to *run, run, run!*

I know who called me. That rasping voice filled with the threat of revenge could only be Victor.

My small Sig Sauer lives in another drawer, always loaded. The cool weight settles into my palm. I switch off the safety and set off on a jerky walk around the house, checking locks, closing the sliding door that leads to the deck, and arming the security system. I search each room, gun first, and deconstruct every shadow.

I end up in the kitchen. I keep my gun close, safety still off. The trees between me and the river sway, sending shadows flickering across the glass panes of the French doors. Any moment, I expect the dark shapes to morph into a six-foot-something hitman with a cruel smile. But they never do.

He's not here. Of course, he isn't. He's not a bogeyman haunting me.

He's not dead, either, apparently. A part of me hoped he wasn't. Another shameful part conjures him up regularly as a nighttime companion. In the hours between sleeping and waking, my subconscious recalls the orgasms he gave me and makes new fantasies. I wake throbbing with arousal and stroke myself to completion, always with Victor's name on my tongue when I come.

Try as I might, I haven't been able to exorcize him completely. And now he's called me.

I'm safe here. Royal equipped this place with the best of the best. He posted a guard for a while before I argued that two dark-haired men lurking in the driveway would draw more attention from the wealthy neighbors than a stand-offish single woman living alone. I promised to be careful.

Then I took him to the range and showed him my shooting scores, and he finally backed off.

Dusk falls. I eat my dinner of yogurt and a handful of walnuts at the kitchen counter, watching the sun's golden fingers stretch across the water, slowly losing its battle with the oncoming night.

I realize I'm rubbing my chest and drop my hand. I miss my sword necklace. I could replace it, but I want my old one back.

I drink a glass of water, then give in to my cravings and open a bottle of wine. A brassy merlot, bold enough to wash the rest of my jitters away.

My phone rings again. I jump ten feet into the air before I realize it's my real one.

"Royal," I answer. "Checking in so soon?" We had a phone meeting only this morning.

"I can't check in on my favorite cousin?" His voice is warm. He's always happier at night after he's been home for a few hours with his wife.

"Oh, so now I'm your favorite? You only say that because I negotiated that deal right from under the Vesuvi's nose."

"I poured some prosecco to celebrate."

"I've got my red wine." I hold up my glass in an unseen toast. "But don't expect the deal to hold them."

"I do not. The best way to deal with the Vesuvi is blunt force. But you have a knack for legal warfare." There's a long pause, and I know the subject he's going to broach next. "Lula, we've spoken of this before—"

Here it comes. I take a big swallow of merlot.

"But it's been long enough. It's time for you to accept your rightful place."

"A woman can't be consigliere. The men won't have it." If

my father was alive, he'd be turning purple at the mere thought of all the work I do for La Famiglia.

"It's a new day. Our fathers are gone." Mine is dead, and Royal's is as good as dead, stuck in prison.

"There'll still be pushback."

"Who's afraid of pushback? You?"

I bite back my automatic response. Royal knows how to push my buttons. I'm already doing the work of a consigliere without the official recognition and a seat at the table. But something holds me back.

"We are not our fathers," Royal continues. "We must forge ahead."

He's right. I can't give him a logical reason for my refusal. How can I explain that I'm still bound to and eaten alive by the past? I can't lie to him, but I can't tell him the truth.

I'm saved by an unusual sound, one that sends alarm prickling up my spine. The whisper of gravel crunching in the driveway outside.

I set down my wine and grab my gun in the same second, my body tense and focused. "Hang on, someone's coming."

"Stay on the line," Royal orders.

"Will do." I didn't get a chance to tell him about the call from Victor. Royal doesn't even know about the burner phone. An oversight? Or some stupid desire to try to keep a piece of Victor to myself?

A thick line of trees surrounds the house, screening me from my neighbors on either side. The yard is full of delicate Japanese maples, and there's a flash of bright orange between the leaves. "Never mind. It's only Gino." My younger brother.

Royal curses in Italian.

"Yeah. I'll tell him."

"Call me after." He hangs up, and I put the safety on my gun before disarming the security system and unlocking the door.

"I almost shot you," I call to Gino. He's parked his car—a Halloween-orange Corvette, not conspicuous at all—at an angle in the driveway, taking up two whole car spaces and blocking the nondescript gray sedan Royal lent me with the house. Not that I need to drive anywhere. Once a week, I give my grocery list to Enzo, Royal's right-hand man, and he sends an underling to bring me whatever I need to survive another week.

He stomps up the stairs, his hands empty. Of course, they are. He never brings me anything. Whenever Royal comes, he brings baskets full of baked goods—raspberry scones, chocolate cupcakes, even tricolored Neopolitan rainbow cookies, when his wife is feeling fancy.

Gino wasn't raised to give. He only takes.

I turn and walk further into the house without greeting him. He finds me in the kitchen, pouring myself more wine. To speak to Gino, I'll need it.

"You shouldn't have come," I say without looking up. "My answer's still no."

"Lula." A grown man's voice shouldn't have such a needling edge or childish whine. "I need it."

"That trust isn't yours. Papa set it aside to care for the house." Probably for this exact reason. "You got the lion's share of the inheritance. Have you spent it already?"

He scowls, and I know the answer. With dark hair and dark eyes, his features are graceful while still being masculine. He's too handsome for his own good. It's gotten him further in life than it should. Being a man in a man's world gets him the rest of the way, but leave it to Gino to want more.

"Call Royal." I feel mildly bad about making my younger brother Royal's problem, but Gino will actually listen to the head of the family. "Ask him for a job."

Gino checks my fridge like he's a teenager in his parents' home. He plucks out a yogurt and stares at it like it's poison before putting it back. He slouches around, poking in empty breadbaskets, but I keep the kitchen empty of temptation. I have a hidden chocolate stash, of course, but anything Royal brings me gets eaten right away.

"Can we order a pizza?"

"Giovanni. No. This is a safe house." I wave my arms. Most of the time, I eschew the whole Italian "talk with my hands" cliche, but Gino brings out the worst in me. "The whole point of this place is to hide. Which is why you can't just show up here whenever you want."

"Can you talk to Royal for me?"

"You're a grown man."

"He gives me grunt work. He doesn't respect me."

"Getting your big sis to speak for you is a sure way to earn it." My voice is as dry as my merlot. "Look, Gino, being family only gets you so far. You have to start from the bottom and work your way up."

"You didn't."

"I went to law school." Again, with the hand waving. Anything to drive my point into my brother's stupid, beautiful head. "And even then, I had to work my way up." How many hours did I spend doing grunt work for the senior partners? I can't explain one hundred-hour work weeks to Gino. He couldn't compute.

I'm rubbing the bare spot above my breasts again.

Gino pouts. It was cute when he was younger, but a man of his age shouldn't do it. "But you–"

A slight breeze has me throwing up a hand to interrupt

Gino and turning to spot the source of fresh air. I shut and locked every door earlier. "What's that?"

I head to the front hall and curse. The front door is wide open. "Gino, what part of 'safe house' do you not understand?" I slam the door and lock it. I hover my finger over the screen pad of the highly sensitive alarm system but don't set it. Knowing Gino, he'll decide to walk onto the deck and set it off accidentally. I'll wait to arm it until after he's gone.

"Of all the stupid, idiotic—yes, I know those are synonyms—things to do, you—" I return to the kitchen, but Gino is gone.

"Gino?"

No answer. It's like he disappeared. Probably poking around, looking for the hard liquor. He's good at finding what he wants when he puts his mind to it.

I grab my glass and swig some wine. Night has fallen, and the house is full of darkness. I usually keep most of the lights off, and I've never felt like the inky corners were hiding anything sinister.

Tonight is different. I'm still on high alert from the phone call and Gino's surprise visit. I flip on the overhead, brighter kitchen lights. That's when I notice the counter is empty. My Sig Sauer is gone.

He's here.

Victor has come for me.

7

L*ula*

I WHIRL and race to the safety of the front entrance.

I sense rather than hear an explosion of movement behind me, the shadows separating, convalescing, becoming a man. Becoming Victor.

The door looms ahead of me. I'm so close. Five more steps, and I'll hit the alarm. Then I'll unlock the front door and escape to safety.

Three more steps. Two. One—

A strong arm wraps around my front, wrenching me back against my attacker's giant frame. I struggle but am pinned. My bare feet kick ineffectively.

A deep voice purrs in my ear. "Vera. Or should I say, *Lucrezia.*"

The bottom falls out of my stomach.

He knows. He knows my real name.

He knows everything.

There's a story among hunters that the instant prey knows it's about to die, it surrenders. I mean to fight, but something in me relaxes against my captor. Recognizing the rightness of his embrace.

But no. I need to fight. Before I start thrashing in earnest, something pricks my neck. A needle. I'd slap at it like a stinging insect, but I'm clamped in Victor's hold. In the next second, darkness rushes over and pulls me under.

I HEAR a leaky faucet somewhere nearby. Water falling from a great height into an empty sink. In the dead quiet of the room, each drop lands with a sound as loud as a gong. *Plink. Plink. Plink.*

That's why it's called water torture. Grab a prisoner, restrain him, and wear him down.

I blink and blink, but my surroundings are nothing but fuzzy shapes. A bright light overhead. A cold, hard, flat surface underneath me. I go to move, but my ankles and wrists are tethered. I'm splayed like da Vinci's Vitruvian Man, all my vulnerable bits exposed.

A shadow falls over me, and I flinch, but there's nowhere to go. I might as well be a corpse, dead on a slab.

I probably will be one shortly. Right now, my cousin Royal is tearing through the safe house. Will he find Gino? Or Gino's body? I do feel regret. I didn't do enough to protect my brother.

Never mind that my brother is a grown man, and I'm in a worse predicament than him. My future promises to be full of blood, bright lights, and lots and lots of pain.

The shadow over me hasn't moved. It's a source of

warmth, though, and part of me wants to strain closer. "Drink," Victor rasps and sets something at my lips. A straw. I suck down liquid because my throat is screaming for it. Too late, I realize that he could be drugging me again. But no, if he wanted to drug me, he'd just stick another needle in my neck. There's a certain cold logic to fatalism. I can guess well enough why I'm here.

I shot Victor, and now he's kidnapped and taken me somewhere he can make the rest of my life painful and very short.

It makes sense. *He who lives by the sword...* I've planned my life around the arc of vengeance, and now here I am, helping someone else complete their own revenge arc.

The water helps clear my vision. Victor stands over me. His white-blond hair is longer now but does nothing to soften the harsh perfection of his sharp features. Only the lush curve of his lips keeps him from looking alien with all of his pointy angles. His lips are soft, too, if I remember correctly. The way they grazed my skin—

Despite my chilled limbs, warmth curls through me. Then I meet his arctic gaze and freeze again.

He studies me like a scientist would study a beetle pinned to a card. There's a certain tenderness in the way he wipes a spilled drop of water from the corner of my mouth. But maybe it's practical instead of kindness. Wouldn't want your victims to die of something as banal as dehydration when there are plenty of more interesting ways to torture them to death.

As soon as I can speak, I croak, "You're alive."

"Yes." He moves so his face is in shadow, and there's no emotion in his voice. Not that he lets much show on his face. "Despite your best efforts."

"So am I." I raise my head and look around. I'm naked,

my body shockingly tanned in this cold, sterile place. The cuffs encircling my wrists and ankles are steel half circles that look sautered right to the table. The room is long and low-ceilinged, without windows, and only white walls, silver cabinets, and glaring fluorescent lights. Like a lab. "You haven't killed me." *Yet.*

Victor steps away, and the harsh overhead light blinds me. I turn my head and blink rapidly. My brain is scrambling to figure a way out of this.

He's fully dressed, of course, in simple slacks and a T-shirt that's nondescript in a stealth-wealth sort of way. All black. A good color to hide blood.

How many victims have died in this room? I inhale, but I only smell cleaning chemicals. Sanitation, the professional murderer's best friend.

"Why would I kill you?" He touches me then, wrapping a long, graceful finger around my ankle. My heart leaps, every cell in my body straining towards his touch, his warmth. I'm laid out like a cadaver, but his touch reminds me I'm alive.

He strokes the inside of my leg like I'm an object he acquired at great expense. "There's no fun in that."

"So you're not going to kill me, then?" I try to scoff, but my voice wavers.

"Do you want to die?"

"Everyone dies." My answer comes too quickly. He removes his hand.

"No, beautiful. You will not die tonight."

One night. I have one night. My heart beats a sad, fragile rhythm like a moth with broken wings fluttering toward a light.

I seduced him once. Could I do it again? My body suddenly thinks that's why we're here. All it took was

Victor's touch and his delicious scent. It's not cologne; it's just him. A fresh, sexy cocktail of pheromones perfectly calibrated to entice me.

My core throbs with a second, shadowy beat. A wave of lust turns my nakedness and my bound wrists and ankles into a kinky game.

I take a deep breath and let it roll through me, elongating my torso and arching my breasts. I lick my lips, ready to speak, but he beats me to it.

"No, my little liar. I'm not going to kill you. I'm going to break you."

Victor

Lucrezia Romano, daughter of Giovanni and Vera Romano, scion of the Regis family. A mafia princess by birth. A lawyer by training. *Lula* to her family.

My prisoner. She lies on my table with her silky dark hair pooled around her head. A Madonna in repose, but for her sharp gaze flitting around the room. Searching for escape. Naked and bolted to the table, she is still mentally throwing herself against the walls of her cage. Figuring out her next steps.

I will have to stay ten moves ahead to win this game. She is my equal in every way. The bullet she put in my belly is proof of that.

The healed wound in my gut twinges as I move around the table.

"Break me? What do you mean?" She looks up at me through her lashes.

I grip her face and let my thumb stroke the line of her

jaw. "Oh no, beautiful. I know your tricks. You will not make me forget myself again."

She quivers like a rabbit. A small part of me wants to unlock the steel cuffs and gather her close. Shush her until she relaxes in my arms.

I've never had such weakness around anyone before. It is a novel sensation.

Another part of me knows she's playing a part, allowing me to see what emotions she wants me to see—the better to bend me to her will. But I have too many elaborate plans and ways I will wreak my revenge.

"How will you break me?"

"You want to know my plan? Do I owe you the truth? Vera?"

Her dark eyes turn flinty. "Did you expect me to give you my real name?"

"What was the name on the marriage certificate? Fake?"

After a moment, she nods.

"No wonder I turned up so little information on you. It should have been a clue to do more research." I wind my hand in her hair, wrapping the silky skein around my palm until I tug her head to the side. "Oh, beautiful, what am I to do with you?"

"You could let me go."

"So you can run out and right into danger? What were you thinking, cornering Stephanos like that? In his lair with his strength at its fullest? And with only a few guns and no backup?"

With me pinning her hair, she can't look at me, but she smiles at the wall, all serenity. "That's exactly what my cousin asked me. It seemed like a decent course of action at the time."

I move my hand, shaking her gently. "You're too smart to believe that. You will tell me the truth."

She blows out a breath. "All right then. It seemed like the only way."

"That's why you seduced that man, David. You wanted to use him to get to Stephanos. It would have worked if he hadn't been embezzling money." I can imagine her strapping the gun under her wedding dress. So much scheming just to put a bullet in Stephanos' head. "You picked an idiot for your plan."

"I know." Her raised voice bounces off the walls. "That's why I rushed Stephanos the next morning. I didn't work so hard, get so far, for it to just end."

"Is that what you thought when I took you? That you had another way in?"

She's silent. It's true.

I knew I was a means to an end, but it still annoys me. The most memorable night of my life and she offered me nothing of herself. Only her body. And in the morning, she walked away.

She won't walk away again so easily.

"Well, now you're over your head, little liar. And the only thing that will save you is how well you obey."

She closes her eyes.

She thinks I am going to torture her. And I am. But not in the way she thinks.

I turn to survey my tools, my weapons of delicate destruction. My knives are honed to perfection, and I have a bevy of new items bought specifically for her. I was trained by a butcher. I know exactly how to draw and quarter and dissect someone.

Grooves around the table edges will allow any blood to

drain away, and when I'm working, I keep a large sheet of plastic underfoot. Easier for clean up.

I didn't lay the plastic down this time. I don't need it. There are subtler ways of mutilating someone.

When I turn back, she's opened her eyes again.

"One question. The man at the house when you took me…" She hesitates, perhaps trying to figure out how long I have kept her. Down here, there is no day or night. This deprivation is part of the plan to break her. "He was my brother. Is my brother. Is he…?"

"Alive. At least, that's how I left him. If he's since rolled his garish sports car off a cliff, it is out of my hands."

"Fair enough. Let's get this over with." She sets her face in a stoic mask, ready for the worst.

She has no idea what I intend to do with her. The depths I will drag her down to. I've spent every waking moment since we met obsessing over her. I won't be content until she has repaid those moments with her own time.

I rap the metal table and hold up a hand in a signal I'll use to cue her to give me her attention. "This is my workshop. This room is soundproof." Well insulated against my victim's screams. It also has its own heating and cooling system. A sink. A shower. And a few feet away from me, in a corner she can't see, a pallet in a cage.

She cranes her head to take half the room in. "Looks like Frankenstein's lab."

"And you will be my new creation. For the time being, this is your home. Eventually, you will earn a better one, as well as a place in my bed."

"How will I earn it?"

I select my first torture implement and hold it up to the light to inspect it. I let the metal catch the light and flash it around the room for her to see. "First, you scream for me."

8

L*ula*

Victor sets down the tool he was holding, something silver and vicious-looking. When he trails his fingers up and down my torso, I'm so on edge that I flinch from his comforting touch.

"Shhhh," he shushes me. "We'll start off easy."

"I bet you say that to all your victims." How many people has he had on this table to carve into until they beg for death?

He fondles my breasts, and I close my eyes again, goose-bumps prickling over my body.

"No, beautiful. You will want to watch this." He holds up what looks like small silver tweezers in one hand while the other rolls my nipple between his thumb and forefinger. Then, he clamps it with the tweezer's padded end. Pain bites into me and subsides almost immediately. I clench my jaw.

Is it better to holler loudly now and pretend I'm more sensitive than I am?

No, I decide, watching him study me and stroke my chest, tracing the spot where my sword necklace used to lie. He wants my real responses. Faking it will make him angry.

Not that this is a game I can win. I've calculated my odds of survival at less than ten percent.

He clamps my other nipple and reaches under the table. There's a whirring sound, and the table starts to rise. Victor waits for it to finish its movement, stroking my leg. His fingers find the raised edge of my most recent scar, and I suck in a breath.

He reaches down and stops the table from moving, leaning down to study the slight scar on my thigh.

"What is this?" he murmurs, almost to himself. "Who hurt you?" He raises his head, making it clear the question was aimed at me.

"It was stupid." I shake my head and remember his admonishment to be truthful. "My one souvenir from the shootout with Bruno." A reminder that I got so close to Stephanos only to fail. "There were chairs and tables in the way, and in all the shooting, there was shrapnel." It wasn't even a bullet. It was a splinter.

I admit this to Victor, but he doesn't laugh. He nods, looking thoughtful.

"I misjudged him," I admit. "Stephanos. I never knew he'd have men who'd be so loyal."

"Ah. Yes. Bruno. He is loyal. Like a puppy you raise to tear out men's throats but also to eat from your hand."

He touches the button under the table, and it continues to rise before tipping forward. I'm on an incline with my head higher than my feet, my weight supported by the steel table and little metal platforms under my heels. With the slight pull of gravity, the tweezer clamps hang from my nipples.

Victor takes a moment to toy with them. "Easy, right?" He unclamps my first nipple, and I suck in a breath. Blood flows back into the tender bud. "Now, let's try these." He holds up a new pair of wicked-looking clamps with tiny screws on one end and little chains on the other. Each chain is tipped with a tiny black jewel. "They're not as bad as the clover clamps. We'll work our way up to those."

He leans in close, his breath caressing my face as he clamps me. First, he twists my nipples this way and that, lifting my full breasts until my back arches off the table. I should hate being manhandled like this, but something about his intense attention mesmerizes me. Every touch stokes the heated longing deep in my core. I try to fight it, but it's inexorable, like a rising tide.

It's a relief when he's finished. He plays with the dangling jewels, then tightens the screws. The sharp sting steals my breath.

"Too much?" He watches my expression. "Breathe through it." He drops his hand, stroking the tops of my thighs. "Vera. Breathe."

"Don't call me that." I almost laugh. "That was my mother's name."

"All right, then. Lula." He purrs my nickname. I've never heard anyone speak it outside of family. It sounds different on the lips of a man who's been inside me. A melodic rise and fall, a line of a song. "You must breathe for me. Otherwise, you might lose consciousness, and what's the fun in that?"

"I thought you'd like me unconscious. Or dead."

"The dead feel no pain." He tightens the screws another millimeter. "What do you know of endorphins?"

"Feel-good chemicals. The body's response to pain."

"Natural morphine. The body releases a load at a time. A round of pain, another load. More time, an increase in pain, another load." Another turn of the screws. My belly is taut as if that will help disperse the sting. "Eventually, you will grow high from it. That is where you will be malleable to me." He puts his face close to me, nuzzling my cheek like a lover. "I will take you to the edge of what you can endure, again and again. Then, I will stretch your limits until you can take more."

"How?"

"Like this." And he puts his hand on my pussy.

Goosebumps break out all over my body. His soothing touches do their job, filling me up with liquid arousal. I'm wet for him. Despite myself, I flex my hips and push into his palm.

"That's it." He rewards me with a little rub. He knows just how to touch me, where to slide his fingers to collect my juices and scratch the itch that awakens more need in me. His lips brush my jaw, their softness belying the cruelty of the clamps. I'm stretched between multiple points of sensation—his kisses, his touch, the stinging pain in my nipples. Suspended between heaven and hell.

He drops his head and sucks lightly on my neck. His fingers grow more insistent, pressing into me. He uses his thumb and forefinger to rub my inner and outer walls until I'm shaking. When he withdraws his fingers, I whimper.

He brushes my clit. "Shall I clamp you right here?" I shudder, and he soothes me. "I could make it feel good."

I bite my lip to keep from begging. I'd rather him cut out my tongue than loosen it.

If I were honest, truly honest, I'd tell him that I don't

want the highs, the ecstasy. I don't want to crave him. I want this to hurt.

"Or I could use a binder clip," he offers. "Make you scream. Wait for you to go numb and then pull the clip off very slowly."

My knees buckle. As I fall, he drives his fingers into me, holding me up like a puppet. He wrenches an orgasm from me this way, brutally stretching me while kissing me softly.

I snap my teeth on his upper lip and bite until I taste blood.

He releases me and plugs my nose until I unclench my jaw. I lick his blood from my lips, spread it across my teeth and give him a bloody grin.

His eyes are icy slits. "Very well. We'll do this the hard way."

~

Victor

My captive looks like a superheroine, beautiful and defiant, with her glossy hair spilling over her shoulders. She's still halfway upright, tilted backward so her weight is on the table, not the steel bonds.

She's so lovely like this. The only thing I'd add is the necklace she used to wear. The one I sleep with every night.

Maybe if she's good, I'll return it to her.

I check her limbs to make sure her circulation is all right while she glares at me. My lip throbs, and there's a distant echo in my gut.

"Okay?" I press my thumb to the tip of my forefinger,

creating a crooked O. In time, she'll learn this unspoken signal means *Okay* or *Go ahead.*

She salutes me with her middle fingers.

"Still not ready to obey," I say with satisfaction. I'd hoped she'd fight. Fighting is ninety percent of the fun.

She bares her teeth at me. They're still stained red.

I select a flogger and snap it. I bought all these toys for her and tested their impact against my own thighs. I start small, flicking the flogger so it lands lightly on her chest and belly, bringing a flush to her skin.

"Is that all you got?" She sounds bored.

I finish with the red flogger and swap it for a black one with heavier strands. I let it fall in waves, focusing on painting her red. There's a clock on the far wall, in my line of sight only. I time myself, finding a rhythm and counting down the moments until her body hits a threshold and releases an endorphin load. The only sound is the impact of the leather, a constant, thrumming rain. Her eyelids grow heavy. Both of us are breathing heavily but also more deeply and in sync.

When I pause to check her, running my hands over her heated limbs, her lips part in a sigh. She wakes up a little when I check her pussy, whining a little when I slide a single digit into her soaked channel. Not enough to push her to orgasm, just enough to stimulate her. I remove my finger and lick it clean.

She's ready for more pain.

I use the same black flogger, but this time, I snap the strands so they bite her sides. She arches her back, mouth open in a silent cry. This is just how I imagined her, night after night. Lula naked, at my mercy, succumbing to sensation. The fantasy got me through months of convalescence. The only thing missing now is the stark red lipstick.

The flogger bites her breasts, leaving faint red lines. She'll look like she swam in a sea of jellyfish.

She has silvery stretch marks on her thighs. I target them next.

Depending on the angle and force of the flogger strands, I can make the hits sting, prick like a volley of needles, or let them soothe the skin, drumming down in a rhythmic rain. I cycle through this, increasing intensity and then backing off. Her mouth is lax and soft, lips parted to suck in more air. Her eyes are almost closed.

There's nothing in the world beyond her prone body—the heat shimmering off her, the sweat rolling down her back. A twitch of her eyebrow. I am made and remade in the rise and fall of her chest.

Even when I work to master her, it's me who is in thrall.

I step close, scenting the sweet bloom of her arousal, and stroke her. She hums a sigh, letting her head loll.

"You're doing so well. Good girl."

Her black brows knot. A part of her wants to reject the compliment. She'll come to crave them in time.

I twist the screws on her nipple clamps tighter, watching the tiny muscles in her face jump.

Another round of flogging, another turn of the screws. There's sweat beading on my back now. My shoulders are warm with the heat of a good workout. My cock is an iron bar, hanging awkwardly down my leg. I run the hard ridge of my palm down my length, savor the painful pleasure, and get back to work.

I let the flogger cleave her psyche open, filling her world with pain. She'll be awash with it, full to the brim, and floating on the ocean until the golden tide of her neurotransmitters transforms the sensation into euphoria. Agony to ecstasy in the span of a simple flogging.

I have many plans for her. Ropes, chains, blindfolds and bindings, even a cage. But all these serve one purpose, one end. Surrender.

She's close. We're nearing the end. I drop the flogger and return to her side to stroke her reddened flesh. Her skin glows with heat, singeing my palms, and her flesh is raw enough that the kindest touch is cruel. I croon to her as I give the screws a final twist, letting her poor, abused nipples feel the maximum pinch of the spring-loaded teeth. She hums a moan but endures.

I check her vitals and give her more water before returning to my row of implements to choose my final weapon. A dragon tail.

The black leather cracks like lightning and bites like the serpent. I let the pointed end taste her skin over and over in increasingly painful pops. She shouts and writhes, but when I step close to admire the blooming red roses on her skin, her pussy gushes into my hand. I tease her until she's panting but pull away before she goes over the edge.

Time for my finale. I crack the whip and flick the nipple clamp off her right breast. Her body snaps upward like she's a puppet, and someone cut all but the middle string leading from her navel. Her cries are high and breathy. I wait until she comes down to let the dragon tail bite one more time and send the left nipple clamp flying. Her heels thrum against the table, an orgasm surging through her like an electric shock.

I drop the whip.

"Lula, are you with me?"

I squeeze her fingers and wait until she presses mine in return. "You did so well, my beauty." I lay a hand on her stomach, and she shudders so prettily. I can't take it anymore. I shove my pants open and take myself in hand.

She's dazed, floating in subspace now. I lean in and lick her tortured right breast. She draws a juddering breath, and I switch to the left one, my tongue circling her tender nipple. Her unhappy mewl only spurs me on. It's not until she lets out a sob that the pleasure gathered at the base of my spine breaches the dam. I let the orgasm take me and spurt my seed over her reddened flesh. I collect some and paint her lips with it. She's earned this much.

"You'll have to earn my cock," I tell her and am gratified by the flicker of disappointment in her eyes.

9

Lula

I FLOAT in a haze of nothing. My eyes are open, but the images are blurred and unfocused, like I'm looking at the world through rain-spattered glass. I reach for my anger, my readiness, but it slips through my fingers. My own body drugged me as effectively as Victor did with a needle earlier today. Or was it yesterday?

Water laps at my legs, washing my scourged flesh. It hurts and soothes, much like everything Victor's done to me.

My captor has me in his arms. I'm taller for a woman, with strong thighs and an ample backside, but next to Victor, I'm petite. I feel every inch of the height difference between us.

Together, we sink into the bath. He's got me cradled close, and for once, I'm grateful for his proximity. My strength is gone. If he wasn't holding me, I would slip under the water and drown.

I don't know how long we soak together. The bath is Roman style, big enough to fit Victor one and a half times or one of him and all of me. There's a bright flash of metal in the corner of my eye, but I am too limp and wrung out to wince at the intimidating sight of the straight razor. He sets it to my ankle, and it takes me a moment to realize that he's shaving me.

I have thick, dark hair and splurged for laser hair removal for my underarms but didn't bother treating anywhere else. If I want my legs smooth, I have to shave them practically every other day.

He shaves me carefully, drawing the blade up my leg in smooth strokes. I keep as still as possible, resigned to my fate.

Other than a few blotches, the red on my shins and thighs has quickly faded to pink. My breasts bore the brunt of his punishment.

I didn't know I could cum from pain.

But I don't want to think about that.

I lick my lips. He's given me plenty to drink, but it takes a few tries to find my voice. "What time is it?"

"Late. Or early."

"You're not going to tell me."

He raises his hand in my line of sight, presses his fingers together and makes a chopping motion. "You don't need to know." He smooths his hand over my knees, the razor following in the wake of his touch. "You don't need to know anything, sweet Lula, except how to please me."

I scoff, but I know he's right. I'm becoming attuned to the shift in his moods and his postures. I will study him like the prey studies the hunter if it means my very survival.

His dick is hard under my backside as he parts my legs, guiding the razor over my sensitive inner thighs. I'm breathing faster now.

"It's all right," he murmurs. "I'll be gentle." And he is. With deft and nimble movements, he shaves my pussy bare. Is it my imagination, or does his knife linger a moment over my femoral artery? One easy slice, and I'd bleed out in his arms.

But then his fun will be over. I have the feeling his plot for revenge has only just begun.

"Why knives?" I ask because I'm too high from my orgasms to keep my barriers up. Which I'm sure is what he counted on.

"Why not?" He sounds amused. "They're strong yet versatile. Simple, easy to hide. People use them every day but forget how deadly they are. But if they handle them too carelessly. . ." He holds up the blade and presses it to his thumb, shaving a layer of skin from the callouses there. "They exact a price."

"But. . . why not a gun?"

"You prefer guns, don't you, my lethal little one?" He kisses my temple and sets the blade at my pussy, angling it to scrape away the dark hairs there. I try not to breathe.

"They're expedient," I say when I can.

"Who taught you to shoot? Your father?"

"No. My father didn't approve at first." I'm distantly aware I'm spilling too much information, but the bridle I keep on my tongue is long gone. "But there was no stopping me. I made one of my uncle's men take me to the shooting range until my father relented and gave me a gun."

"He didn't encourage you?"

"He thought it was amusing." My voice is hard.

"He underestimated you."

"Yes." Like every other man in my life. Except Royal. And now, maybe Victor.

"And now you are an excellent shot."

"I missed Stephanos."

"You got closer to him than anyone has. He's better at hiding and surviving than anything else."

"So I've heard." This is why my father and uncle gave up on avenging my mother decades ago. Until I learned the truth of her murder and decided to do it myself. "And it still wasn't good enough."

"Do not punish yourself." He sets the blade aside with a clink and palms my bare pussy. His lips find my ear. "That is for me to do."

His long, skilled fingers glide up and down my sex, drawing out threads of arousal.

"Did your fiancé ever touch you like this?"

I can't stop my sharp laugh. "David? No. I never even let him touch me. How do you think I got him to the altar so quickly?"

Victor hums and touches me more, taking what I've refused to give any lover. I try to stay his hand, and he captures my wrists with his large left hand, keeping his right one free to rub me. Under the thick blanket of fatigue, my pussy throbs under his touch. My orgasm threatens.

I rock my head from side to side, resisting. "No. . ."

"Yes. Just one more, Lula. And then I'll let you rest. I'll be done with you for at least a little while."

The hard cock under my ass says otherwise, but I have no choice. I melt into the strong cage of his body and allow him to wring another round of climaxes from my exhausted body.

I WAKE on my back and raise my head. I'm still in Victor's murder dungeon, with the same gray shadows and dim lights. The long, steel rods of my enclosure separated me from the rest of the room, but I slept comfortably for being in a cage.

I'm on a soft pallet directly on the concrete floor. There's no blanket, but it's warmer now than the night before. Or maybe my naked flesh is still warm from the flogging and bath.

There are no windows or natural light. No sign of what day or time it is. No way of knowing how long I slept.

The memory of last night comes back to me, and I squeeze my eyes shut. His big, capable hands guided the knife over my slick, sensitive flesh, shaving me. Baring me. I was sensation-drunk, and he knew just how to touch me. He could've asked anything of me, and I probably would've done it.

I need to shore up my defenses against him, but I have no idea how.

It's not the pain I'm afraid of. It's the orgasms. And his prying mind, slicing open my psyche, seeing and cataloging every hope and desire.

I sit up, and Victor immediately appears in his psychopath-relaxing-at-home outfit of loose black clothing. His feet are bare as he squats to come to eye level with me.

"Did you sleep well?"

"Yes, thank you," I reply automatically. The side of his mouth draws up at my politeness, but I figure it can't hurt to be courteous. Until I figure out a way to kill him.

"Any pain?" His gaze lingers on the red blotches on my chest.

I shrug. "I'm sore. Like a mild case of sunburn."

"Very good." He makes the *Okay* symbol with his thumb and pointer finger. "You will tell me if the pain is too much."

I barely stop myself from rolling my eyes. "So you can hurt me more?"

He clucks, angling his head to the side so the light lovingly highlights the planes of his beautiful face. "I do not want you to hurt all the time. Only when I wish it."

"Right." I glance down at my naked self. My shaved pussy looks paler against the rest of my skin. Humiliation is a bitter taste in my mouth, but what's worse is how my pussy pulses, aching to be filled. His cruel smile, the sexy rasp of his voice, his perfect face fills me with need. He's a monster holding me captive, I shouldn't feel this way.

He smirks down at me as if he knows what I'm thinking. How part of me likes being naked and helpless in contrast to his powerful, clothed form. As if he knows the depths of my desire for him.

Rage surges within me, and I stoke it, needing its heat. "Do I get clothes?"

"When you earn them." He offers me a bottle of water, already unscrewed, with a straw sticking out of the top. I reach for it, and he shakes his head, holding it for me and praising me like I'm a wild animal he's coaxed to drink from his hand. "Good girl." His pointer finger taps his thumb a few times. He's trying to train me with hand gestures, like a dog. I hate it but make a careful note of each one.

I drink the entire bottle, grateful he's not adding water deprivation to the torture routine.

"More?" he offers, and I decline politely, hoping he'll keep me hydrated as needed.

He makes a come hither motion with his four fingers pressed together. Another damn hand signal. "Turn around and put your hands through the bar."

I hesitate.

"Good girls get rewards." Again, he makes two taps with his forefinger on his thumb before reaching behind him for a white paper bag. When he opens it, the scent of fried food wafts over me, and my stomach convulses and growls so loudly that the sound echoes.

"That's from Three Diner."

"Yes. I learned you went there after you. . . left me. But they would not speak to me."

My throat tightens. I fight the vision of a baby-pink uniform spattered with blood. "Did you hurt them?"

"I had no reason to." He motions, and I scoot around and lean against the bars. He grabs my wrists and links them together. I crane my head but can't quite see more than black leather cuffs. They're soft and snug, joined by a short chain. I'm able to relax my arms without wrenching my shoulders. Could be worse.

He has me turn back to him and kneel so he can feed me by hand, one bite of burger at a time.

"Gonna kill me with cholesterol?" I joke between French fries.

"You will need the sustenance," he informs me. My stomach flips at his intent expression, but the trepidation isn't enough to dull my appetite.

After the meal and a little more water, he wipes my face. I look past him to a small sink beside a door. The small room beyond seems to hold a toilet.

Victor catches me looking and raises a brow, waiting for me to ask.

"I need to use the bathroom." I lower my eyes, not sure if I'm feigning humiliation. I'm already naked and kneeling, locked in a cage.

"You can have anything your heart desires." He produces

a black leather contraption—two straps wrapped around a silver ring. "As long as you please me."

He motions me forward with the same *Come* signal and has me kneel up and hold still while he affixes the ring gag. With the straps buckled tight, my lips are rounded into a forced "O," and my heart trips.

"Okay?" he asks, with the corresponding hand signal. I nod. It's that or try to talk around the gag.

Victor shoves his pants down and shows me the beautiful monster of his cock—long and uncut and turgid—and my heart stutters. My mouth is already open, ready for him, and I'm drooling around the metal ring.

The first taste of him is sweet. He glides deeper, spearing my mouth, and I breathe in the wintry scent of him, tasting salt. He reaches through the cage bars to grip my hair and control my movements. "Breath through your nose." His harsh direction is a mercy as he fills me with his length, tipping my head back until he's knocking on the entrance of my throat. My chest surges, and I bite down on the metal until my teeth ache.

"Good, good girl." He eases out, giving me a moment to gasp. He taps his thumb and forefinger together a few times before swiping a thumb at the corner of my eye, collecting my tears. He tastes them and gives me the *Come* signal. "Again."

After a few rounds of this, my knees are aching, but my throat has gone soft enough to let him in. Tears streak down my cheeks, and I let them because they seem to please him. At long last, he presses my head against the bars and spurts down my throat.

"Perfection," he pronounces and massages my face after removing the gag. "You're doing well, Lula."

And despite myself, I feel a stab of pride.

Victor

I have to help Lula upright. I collared and blindfolded her before I allowed her out of the cage. Her nostrils flared like a frightened mare. She's more tense now than she was in her cage, her arm rigid in my grasp. She hates to be out of control.

She'll grow accustomed to this life. Moving gracefully through my home, naked for my pleasure, kneeling as often and for as long as I like, and obeying my hand signal's silent commands. One day, perhaps, she will crawl for me and beg to be caged, to be chained.

I unclip one of her hands and allow her to use the bathroom with the door slightly cracked. The privacy is more than she deserves, considering her history of hiding weapons under sinks. But that was my oversight.

When I tell her time is up and open the door, she doesn't seem grateful.

"How long are you going to keep me like this?" she asks, glaring at me. She's removed the blindfold, a liberty she'll be punished for, but she allows me to secure her free arm behind her.

"It's up to you. My bed is ready for us. But first, I will train you to submit the way I like."

Her lips press together.

"Surrender now. It'll go easier for you." When she doesn't respond, I take her arm and guide her past me. She goes obediently enough but rears back when she sees what's waiting for her.

The steel table is gone from the middle of the room,

pushed to the side and hidden from view. In its place is a Saint Andrew's cross. Made of sturdy dark wood and padded with black leather, the X shape seems to fill the space.

I give her a moment, enjoying the music of her harsh breathing. Then I draw her forward to stand before the cross.

"As long as it takes, Lula. I won't stop until you beg me to make you mine."

10

Lula

I PRESS my cheek to the leather cross. It slips a little because the surface is slick with my sweat. Overhead, my arms sag in their bonds. My back is in flames. Victor warmed me up with a light flogger, then quickly moved to a heavier one. As soon as I got used to the thuddy rhythm of the strands, he changed the angle of the strokes so it felt like stinging rain. He hasn't touched my nipples, but they throb in sympathy with my abused backside.

And now he has a crop. He showed me the implement before tapping it on my calves and the backs of my thighs. He pops it harder on the fleshy swell of my ass, making me growl. The crop peppers my back and rear, leaving spots of fire, and as much as I hate the pain, I love the heat it leaves.

The crop prods the side of my breasts. "Breathe, Lula," he says, and I brace for the sting. The leather flap kisses the side of my left and then right breast. I snarl, straining against my cuffs.

"Smarts, doesn't it?"

"Fuck you," I mutter.

"So impolite. Where are your manners?"

Something wide and rectangular presses against my ass and then claps down harder. I shout. "Oh, you bastard."

Another hard smack to my opposite rear cheek, but I was expecting it. He stops to give me a sip of water, and I glare at him. "Kinky fucker. Do you do this with all your victims?"

"Just you."

"So I'm special."

"Very."

He steps behind me again, a monster looming behind me. Something soft falls on my face, and I rear back.

"Shhh, it's just the blindfold." He draws the strip of silk tight over my eyes, and the world drops away. There's no light, no movement, not even a sense of shapes or shadows. It's darker than night.

I'd rather endure hours of pain than have my sight taken from me this way. I bite my lip to keep from begging.

Victor shifts behind me. I tune into the slight rustle of his clothes and the soft huff of his breathing. He steps closer, his clothing brushing my back, and goosebumps run down my skin.

He runs his hands down my sides, circling the sore weals his crop left on my backside. There's nothing for me to see or focus on except the cool, tickling trail his fingers leave on my skin. It's soothing, inevitable. He takes time stroking down my calves, even my ankles. His touch is gentle, but I tremble, wanting to resist. To fight. He presses himself against my back, awakening the sting and, worse, an intense craving deep in my gut. He slides his hands around my front and traces light circles there. It's sweet and sensual, and my body is confused. Is this my enemy? Or my lover?

"Stop," I whisper. "No."

"No?" He stills, glued to my back from nape to knee. "Not this?" His fingers ghost down the vee of my legs, towards my shaved pussy. "Or this?" The lightest touch on my folds.

I shake my head but can't bring myself to protest.

He drops his lips to my bare shoulder. "It's all right, little liar. But I still need to punish you for removing the blindfold."

He steps away, and I'm filled with relief. Let him beat me, mark me, etch his rage on my skin. Just don't make me like it or crave it.

Don't make me cum.

"Shall I use the flogger?" Soft suede trails over my back. "The paddle? Or the crop? Shall we try something new?"

There's no use answering. Anything I say will make it worse.

I rub my head against the leather, wishing I could dislodge the blindfold.

"Bad girl." He grips my hair and draws my head back. I let him so as not to wrench my neck. "I'll put you in a posture collar if you do that."

More bondage. He's been lenient so far. Things could be so much worse. "I won't," I say. "I'll be good."

"Yes, you will. I know just how to keep you sweet."

He leaves and returns to fit something around my waist and legs. It feels like a harness with a wide section to cover my pussy. Some sort of chastity belt? I'm happy with anything that keeps him from playing with my pussy and giving me pleasure.

He tightens the contraption. I rise to tiptoe but can't escape the panel pressing against me.

"How does this feel?" he asks.

The thing between my legs comes to life, vibrating right against my clit. I yelp and push upwards as if that will allow me to escape it.

"Excellent." He steps away and spends the next interminable minutes adjusting the speed and intensity of the vibrations, finally settling on a swelling buzz that rises and falls in uneven waves. Heat fills my belly but settles at a gentle simmer. Without my vision, there's nothing but the insistent and random stimulation between my legs. I lean against the cross, rubbing my nipples on the sturdy frame in an attempt to get a spark, a sting, something that will trigger my climax.

This is torture of the sweetest kind.

The toy buzzes as he resumes flogging me, and sensations collide until I don't know which is which: the sting in my back, the tickling at my clit, or the tightening in my core muscles. There are no boundaries between them and the rising tide of my climax, threatening to consume me.

I angle my hips, desperate to rub against the cross. If I can push at the panel between my legs and press it closer, I can get some relief. But it's no use. As soon as I push my pelvis forward, Victor stops the vibration.

"Naughty girl." Victor comes to hold my hip and pat me with the paddle again. He swats me until I'm dancing from right foot to left, trying to get away. Then, he amps up the vibrator, transforming the pain to golden and perfect pressure. My clit swells, my orgasm darting just within reach—

The vibration dies.

"No," I mumble, despite myself. "Please."

"Since you ask so nicely. . . beg for your punishment. And I'll give you a reward."

My thoughts trip and fall over themselves. I take too long to answer, and Victor steps away again.

"Very well." He switches to the heavier flogger, letting the strands fall in a wall of knotted ends that knock the breath out of me. The blows leave me numb at first, the pain rushing in too late.

I curse, but eventually, my anger runs out. I'm lost in the darkness, and at least the pain gives me something to focus on. It flares in the distance, a bright, wicked light.

Besides, focusing on the pain lets me ignore what else is happening in my body. Some strange alchemy is happening, transforming all sensations to the deep, insistent ache between my legs.

Eventually, the pain isn't enough to keep me tied to the present. It becomes one giant, surging ocean, and I'm lost in the rise and fall of the waves.

I can't see, but I can hear. Without realizing it, I start to hum. The sound is another vibration, a pleasing counterpoint to the one between my legs.

I barely hear Victor calling my name. His cheek rubs mine, and I lean into the pleasant prick of stubble.

"Still with me?" He cups my breasts and kisses my sweaty neck. I press into his palms and bow my head, letting him trail his mouth over the tender spots. He could cut my throat. He could bite me and make me bleed. Instead, he's kissing me with impossibly soft lips. I want to hate it, but I don't. It feels so good.

When he steps away, I want to cry. I wait for another round of flogging, but nothing comes. The vibrator on my clit surges higher and higher. I pant through it, my hips jutting forward as if I can ride the invisible waves. All too soon, they die away.

"Tell me what you want, beautiful. Tell me, and I'll give it to you."

"Please. I want to cum." My voice sounds far away.

He loosens the harness, and I almost cry. The straps and panel fall away, but in their place, Victor puts his hand.

"Beg me," he hisses. His voice is all malice, but his long fingers are already working between my legs, bringing me bliss.

"Please, please, please," I whisper over and over. It doesn't feel like defeat. It feels right, like the natural next step. Like I've been underwater, finally broke the surface, and it's time to take a sweet inhale. It's not surrender. It's what I need to survive.

He strums my clit just right, pulling my moans out of me like music.

"Yes," I say. "More."

His fingers plunge into my soaked channel. It's almost enough. My orgasm is bright and shining and within reach. And he slips his free hand around my breast and tweaks my sore nipple.

I cum, shaking against the cross, mouth open. Howls fill my ears. As I come down from the peak, I realize the sound is coming from me.

Victor moves close to me, and my arms drop. Victor frees my ankles next and scoops me up. I'm still blindfolded—in the dark and off balance. I grab at him, clinging to my captor like he's the only thing tethering me to the earth.

"I need to taste you."

I'm laid out on a table and strapped down again, but I don't care because my legs are pulled apart, and Victor is there, oh, he's there, and his hot mouth is on my folds, and his tongue presses in. I throw back my head and scream. He licks and probes and devours me, and my orgasm swells again, no gentle tide this time but a tidal wave that's crashing over me, destroying everything in its path.

I can't see anything, and it's cruel. Every squeeze of his hand, every soft swipe of his tongue, is all magnified a millionfold. It's cruel to deny me the sight of Victor's intent face: his mouth hidden by the swell of my sex, his eyes on mine, and his pupils blown, the icy blue of his irises consumed by lust.

I don't know how long he eats me, how many orgasms I have, or whether it was one long, continuous orgasm. I only know that it's a mercy when he finally takes his mouth away.

"Lula," he growls, and the flogger falls again, warming my front. Then it's the crop, biting at my breasts. It hurts and feels good. I arch my back, accepting the pain, feeling the connection to him any way I can. I want to feel him, to touch him. Pain or pleasure don't matter. I want more, more, more.

His thumb nudges my clit, and I realize he's stopped striking me. My body is throbbing. I am scoured by sensation, devoured by it, and every nerve is singing. I imagine my body lying on the padded platform, no metal table this time, my skin a painting of pink and red and my pussy a pale target. I feel Victor lean over me, his pale head at my collarbone, dragging down my breasts. His tongue probes my belly button, and I let out a long, low groan. The barest amount of penetration feels so damn good.

"Do you want me, Lula? In this pretty pussy?" He pets it, and every stroke of his fingers is delicious. "Will you be good for me?"

In the distance, an alarm bell is ringing. Under the silk, I squeeze my eyes shut.

"Good girls get to come on my cock." His fingers slip

down into the cleft of my ass. "Bad girls get something else." The tips find my back hole, tickling the tight skin there. A shock runs through me.

"Has anyone ever taken you here?" He leans close, whispering like a lover. I hold my breath as he circles my rim. I clench my buttocks, but it's no use. He's pressing in, and his finger is so slick from my pussy that he's able to breach the tight ring of muscle. Just a millimeter but it burns. "Have they? Answer me, Lula."

"No."

"I will be your first." He sounds so confident that a tremor goes through me. "Soon." His hand falls away, and I feel relief, but it's short-lived.

He steps away, and the crop falls again, this time on my unprotected pussy. He alternates smacking it and using it to probe my folds. He uses it to work me up to orgasm again, and it's wonderful and awful. When he finally releases me from the table and gathers me into his arms, I cling to him like he's my anchor in the ocean. If I let go, I'll drown.

~

Lula

"Why Stephanos?" We're in the shower after another long session on the table and then the cross. We've fallen into a routine: he ties me up and works me over. Every time he gives me an instruction, he uses the hand signals I've now memorized. I'm made to beg for my orgasm, and then he gives me so many I beg him to stop. I wake up in the cage. I'm fed and watered and allowed some privacy, but he's always near. He bathes me himself, either in the bath or, this time, in the shower. Sometimes, he keeps me blindfolded. And he always keeps me shaved.

There's no more talk of earning privileges, but I know he's keeping track of my behavior. Sometimes when I beg him to stop, he shows mercy and doesn't make me cum. Instead of figuring out how to free myself, grab one of his many knives and plunge it into his heart, I find myself thinking of ways I can please him. And as much as I tell myself that pleasing him will lead to more freedom, which will give me a chance to escape, it's only a partial truth.

He's wearing me down.

"Lula," Victor sing-songs and tweaks my nipple. He's introduced me to the clover clamps, and I've never known such pain. I go to great lengths to keep him happy when I'm wearing them.

What was he asking me? "Stephanos? He's our enemy."

"He's a petty thief compared to the Regis family. A fly buzzing around a pack of lions."

"He's stolen from us."

"He's stolen from all the families. For many years. He's a scavenger. It's not enough to explain your lifelong vendetta."

It seems impossible that Victor doesn't know of my mother's death. It's more likely that he knows and is toying with me, wanting me to bare myself and my reasons to him. "Maybe I don't like thieves."

He smacks my ass. The sound echoes in the tiled space. "You defend them for a living. Don't lie to me." His hand cups my rear, massaging it. "You know I do not allow lies between us." His touch grows bolder, slipping into the crevice of my ass. With a foot, he nudges my feet apart and bows me forward so he can play with my ass. He's been encroaching on this forbidden territory more often, in the deepest part of a pain session when I'm too limp to protest. He pushes his fingers deep into my cleft, finding the slick skin of my seam and massaging. It feels weirdly good. I press my palms against the tile, partly to brace myself and partly to pretend I can push the sensation away.

"You know I'll find out eventually," he taunts, the blunt edge of his knuckle pressing onto my rim. He has long, elegant fingers, but they feel impossibly huge when he works one into my ass.

"If you won't tell me why you went after Stephanos, you will tell me why you ran into danger so recklessly and without backup. Practically unarmed."

"I wasn't—"

"It was stupid." He stops threatening to penetrate my ass and grips it hard, squeezing so tight I'm sure I'll have violet bruises on my skin. "One word and you'd have the full might of the Regis family behind you. And maybe even the other families if you formed an alliance."

I swallowed. I never thought of an alliance. But get too many people involved, and there would be a chance that Stephanos wouldn't die from one of my bullets.

"So why, Lula? Why were you so foolish? I'm sure your cousin would back you up—"

"There's a mole!" My voice rings out, too bright and loud, and I bite my lip to keep from saying any more. Victor's not a judge I have to convince by making my case. He's my captor, and every second, every hour, he worms deeper into my psyche.

"Ah." Victor lets his hand fall away. "A mole. That explains why Stephanos has survived all this time."

"He's a rat."

"Who attracts other rats. Have you uncovered this mole?"

"If I had, I would've had backup. I wouldn't have done something so... so stupid."

"Suicidal." His voice is flat, but he presses himself to my back. I rise, and he grips my hips, pulling me gently against him. He's hard—he's always hard. It takes an inhuman effort to sate him, and he's been holding back during my torture sessions. I arch my back, leaning into him, but he doesn't kick my feet apart and take me. He picks up the soap and lets his hands roam up my chest, sliding over my skin under the pretense of washing me. I hold my breath and let him touch me. It feels wonderful, and I know this is part of his plan to break me. In a minute, he'll drop the soap and take up the straight razor, gliding it over my skin and smoothing my stubble away. There's no part of me that he hasn't thoroughly touched. No part that he doesn't own.

"That was the worst part," he rasps in my ear after a long while. I blink and realize I've drifted off. I'm unsteady on my feet, still leaning against him as the shower beats down in a gentle rain. He must have a massive hot water tank.

"What was?"

"Sitting as the doctor stitched me up, learning you'd wandered into Stephanos' lair wearing nothing but two guns and my coat."

"I wore heels and stockings too," I correct, not wanting him to miss out on the full visual. He plucks my nipples in retaliation, and I welcome the sting. I need something to pull me out of my haze.

"I waited and waited for word of what happened to you."

"Why?"

"You know why."

I could deny that I do, but it's obvious. He wanted me alive so he could kill me himself. Sometimes, when I wake up on my pallet in the cage, I'm surprised I'm still alive.

"And then I learned you were still alive and safe. Secured in the Regis family's stronghold."

"Not so secure," I mutter, remembering how easily he found me.

"There is no fortress that can keep me out. It was only a matter of time." He skates a hand down my front until he cups my pussy. He pushes two fingers into me and tugs forward, roughly massaging my G-spot until my damn body shakes like the last autumn leaf on a branch. "And while I searched for you, I imagined what I'd do to you. How I'd train you to please me."

As his fingers delve deep, stretching me, he rubs the heel of his palm over my clit, frigging me in rough, scrubbing movements. Like my orgasm will be a punishment. With my sex raw from the orgasms he gave me earlier, maybe it will be. "How I'd punish you for leaving. For nearly throwing your life away."

"Not for trying to kill you?"

"No, Lula." He releases my cunt, leaving me on the brink. It's both a relief and a torment. I grit my teeth to bite back my moan. "We both know you didn't try to kill me."

"I shot you."

"In the gut." He takes a handful of my wet hair and tugs my head back. In this position, I'm vulnerable. But it feels good, too, the pinch of pain at my skull from his fist in my hair and the water washing over my upturned face.

His teeth score my throat.

"I've never killed before. Maybe that's why I missed Stephanos." My voice wobbles. After all my practice and long hours at the range, I proved too soft-hearted. Too weak.

"Perhaps. But you didn't miss me. You could've shot me between the eyes. Instant death." He guides my head down so he can take the nape of my neck between his teeth. Like a lion disciplining a lioness. "Or in the heart. But you didn't, did you?"

"Maybe I wanted you to suffer."

"You left your mark on me, but you wanted me to live? Because deep down you knew."

I jerk back, jabbing my elbows into his solid frame. I haven't fought him before, wanting to wait until he's truly off guard, and this isn't a real or very serious attempt. We're both naked in the shower, but he's twice as large as me and more confident in hand-to-hand combat. An elbow in the gut won't incapacitate him, not even if I get lucky and poke him right in his healing wound. My struggles are futile.

But I have to shut him up.

My feet slip on the tile as I push myself away, finding a corner to brace my back in. He's on me immediately, grabbing my wrists as I claw at him, closing in and pinning my legs so I can't kick. I snarl, teeth bared, and he shoves me flush against the wall, my wrists caught in his grip and secured over my head. He's taller than me and monstrously strong, using every inch of his body to trap me. Both of my wrists fit into his left hand, leaving his right one free to collar my neck. In the end, I'm imprisoned between him and the shower tile.

I can't move, but I can glare at him. If looks could kill, he'd be bleeding out. He studies me and smiles, water streaming down his brutally beautiful face. His lips are close to mine. If he tries to kiss me, I'll bite through his tongue.

"You could've killed me," he purrs. "And you didn't. You know why?"

I surge against him and use the little space I gain to twist away from him. He slams me front-first against the tile, his dick jabbing my back. His chuckle echoes around the shower.

"You liked me, Lula. You didn't want me to die."

"You weren't worth another bullet."

He presses into me more, keeping me pinned while he shifts his right hand to get a better grip on my throat. "You hoped I would live. And you knew if I did, I would come for you. A part of you must have wanted it."

"No."

"Do not lie to me." His fingers press in, constricting my airway. I fight but can't move much.

This is it. He's going to kill me. He knows just where to squeeze, to choke me, and I'm helpless, dangling in his arms.

"Admit it," he growls into my ear. "You wanted me."

"No."

"You wanted to return to me."

"No. . ." My voice is growing fainter, my brain screaming for air. I claw at the tile, but I'm getting weaker and weaker. The air is gone from my lungs and, with it, my strength.

"You need to be claimed like this, to be owned." His voice comes from far away.

I'm dying. He's killing me. I'm at the end.

"Lula. . ."

I open my mouth and croak with the ghost of my last breath. "Do it."

"Fuck," he snarls and releases his grip. Sweet, precious air rushes in, and I rise with it like a freed balloon floating into the sky. I'm weightless as Victor lifts me, hitching me up the wall so he can part my legs and slam his cock into my cunt. It feels so good, so right. I'd never taken a man bare before Victor, and it's wrong but perfect.

He fucks me higher and higher, and I come with my head somewhere in the stratosphere, my cheek sliding against the tile.

11

L*ula*

"Lula, stay with me."

There is no Lula. She's gone, eaten up by ecstasy. I don't recognize myself. I barely recognize my own name. There are no boundaries between me and the outside world. Nothing left of my defenses. Victor fucked them away.

A small, primitive part of me recognizes that I'm being dried and carried out of the shower. He fucked me there, choked me, and I welcomed it. I welcomed death.

But he didn't kill me. He shattered me in pieces, and it's fine because I'm not myself anymore.

"Speak to me, little one."

I snort. I'm not that little. I have a slender torso but ample breasts and an even bigger backside. Leah's muffins go straight to my hips. Only hours of rowing keep them off my thighs.

I must say all this out loud because Victor replies, "Noted." He sounds amused. "But you are little to me."

He lays me down, and I sink into the soft, cloud-like surface. He leans over me, a shadowy shape. Victor. The victor in our little game. In our fight to the death.

I should've known it would end like this. With him standing over me, a bloodied knife...

Something prods my lips. A straw. "Drink, beautiful."

I do, and when I'm done, I say, "I'm not beautiful."

He sighs from somewhere overhead. "Must you argue?"

"Yes. I was born to argue. I might as well die doing it."

I'm rolled and wrapped in something fuzzy and warm. A blanket. There are words for so many things, words I already know, but everything's floating just out of reach.

"Enough, sweetheart."

Sweetheart?

"Shhh." Victor tucks the blanket around me. "It's time to rest. I pushed you too far."

Wasn't that the point?

"If you don't stop talking, I will gag you."

I didn't realize I was still talking. My throat is raw. Victor gets me more water and climbs into bed with me. His arms cradle me, pulling me against the solid wall of his body. I close my eyes and let myself drift...

And it occurs to me that I've never been held this close before, not since I was young. Before my mother died, and my world turned cold.

"It was for my mother," I say. "That's why I targeted Stephanos."

"I know."

"I knew it! I knew you knew."

"Yes, little one, you were right." A kiss on my temple.

"He killed her outside of the pasta makers," I tell him.

Words bubble out of me like I'm a bottle of champagne, newly uncorked. "It was meant to look like the Vesuvis did it. But I dug and figured out. . . I found out. . ."

Victor touches me, and I realize my face is wet.

"It was him," I say. My eyes are burning, so I keep them closed. "He wanted to kill her. To incite a war."

"Shhhh."

There's a monster in my chest, clawing out of me, but I finish what I have to tell him. "She was on her way to pick me up from school and stopped to get fresh cavatelli. My favorite." And then it hurts too much. I can't say any more.

A long time later, Victor says. "It's not your fault. You know that, right?"

I don't know anything.

"You're going to be all right, my Lucrezia. You will heal from this."

"You can't tell me what to do." I mold my fingers into the chopping hand gesture in case he doesn't get it. *No.*

His laugh is a gust of wintry wind on my face. "Very well. You will decide for yourself."

That sounds better.

"Now go to sleep. We can argue more in the morning. As much as you like."

I yawn, but I'm suddenly more awake. My pain has leaked away, gone like it's never been. I wiggle my hips, trying to nestle deeper into the bedclothes, only to realize I'm rubbing against Victor. I give up and sigh. "I can't sleep."

"Yes, you can."

"I don't want to. When I wake up, you'll hurt me again."

"Yes. But you like it when I hurt you."

"You're not supposed to know that."

"Is it not obvious?"

I grit my teeth, trying to summon some rage. There's only exhaustion. "You're going to win. And I hate it."

"There is no losing. Not between us."

"It doesn't feel that way." Hovering just overhead is a heavy gray fog. Exhaustion ready to smother me. I hold it back a little longer. "You said you'd break me. And now I'm not me anymore."

"What does that mean?"

"I don't exist. I need to fight. If I'm not fighting, I'm not alive."

"Is that why you hunt your mother's killer?"

It is, but I've never thought of it that way before. The only way I survived that great loss was by committing myself to avenging her death. The goal drove me forward so I would have something to live for.

"You think I'm pathetic."

"No, my Lucrezia. Not that. Never that." He pulls me even tighter to him, tying me to reality even as his warmth threatens to pull me into sleep. "Enough of this. Let me tell you something real."

As I float away, he follows me, telling me the story of a boy who loved knives and lived above a butcher shop and whose mother let the butcher hurt her until the boy grew up and killed him and any other man who would prey upon them. And they lived happily ever after, the end.

Victor

I WAIT A LONG WHILE, dozing on and off with Lula in my arms. After a REM cycle, I slide away, careful not to wake her. There's no worry of that, though. She's sleeping soundly. I take her vitals, and she barely stirs. I email an update to my doctor, the one who patched me up the first time I had Lula as a guest, who's advising me on the sleep/sexual torture protocol I'm cycling her through and helping me keep tabs on her health.

With her dark hair spread over the pillow and black lashes fanned over her tanned cheeks, she looks like an angel fallen to earth. Her lips are plush and pouting, her expression sweeter than she'd allow if she was awake. I trace her brow line, and she frowns as if frustrated by the gentle touch.

I turned up the heat before I climbed into bed with her, but now I lower it and cover her with a weighted blanket so she'll sleep well.

Before I leave, I turn on the camera in the corner that streams an encrypted feed to a private website. The doctor will monitor her while I'm gone. And I can log in and check on her while she sleeps.

I would stay, but I have business to attend to.

It's been three months since Lula surprised Stephanos and wounded him; he's gone to ground where even I cannot find him. Not that I tried too hard. I was more focused on Lula.

But now that I have her secure, it's time for me to collect what I'm owed.

My contacts have traced the remnants of Stephanos' gang to a shuttered hole-in-the-wall restaurant called Primo Pizzeria. I cased the joint two nights ago and set up cameras so I could study the henchmen in their natural territory. I haven't done a complete watch-through of the footage, only a few hours to get a sense of the players and their hierarchy and roles. I will do my homework more thoroughly the next time Lula sleeps, but I have all the information I need for this afternoon's work.

I first approach the Pizzeria from the front. The windows and door are covered in ancient, sun-browned newspapers. I set a sleek black briefcase right on the stoop, slim enough to sit in the shadows and go unnoticed until the proper time.

Then, I retrace my steps and slip up the fetid alley, avoiding crumpled beer cans and cast-off takeout containers. The back door is cracked, and in one silent motion, I ease my way inside.

Gruff voices echo through the empty kitchen. I don't try to hide myself but simply walk into the main seating area, right up to the men lounging in a circle of chairs.

"Good morning," I murmur. Instantly, four of the five men reach to snap their weapons up and train them on me.

The fifth one fumbles his and drops it on the floor. It hits the toe of his tennis shoe and spins across the floor, stopping a few inches from my boot. I raise a brow.

"Who the fuck are you?"

I spread my arms to show I hold no visible weapons. "A friend."

I wait calmly until the wiry, curly-haired man in the center spits out his cigarette and lowers his gun. "Hey, I know you. You're that hitman Stephanos hired to bump the suit."

"Yes. You may call me Victor."

The wiry man narrows his eyes at me for a moment, then relaxes. "I'm Spiro. That's Uzi, Kill Zone, Bruiser, and Joe." He gestures to each of his friends in turn.

"A pleasure." They're all scowling at me with varying degrees of distrust. I raise my bare palms to show my intent. "May I?"

When no one says anything, I bend down slowly and

pick up the gun. "Kill Zone?" I offer it to the man who dropped it. He blinks slowly and takes it.

Uzi still has his weapon trained on me.

"I remember there being more of you the last time I visited," I muse. "Where is the gentleman who drove me from the wedding?"

"That was Johnson," Joe pipes up. He's a big, ugly man wearing a white tank top under an ill-fitting suit jacket. He's broad in the shoulder and tall, but not as tall as Uzi. "Got hit by a bullet in the shootout at Cavalli's. You know, the one with the broad." He mimes a woman opening her coat. He's speaking of Lula, and it's all I can do to keep myself from flicking a knife into his throat.

When I first heard the story of the naked woman who walked into Cavalli's and started shooting, I was filled with both pride and rage. Rage that she would be so reckless. Pride that she could be so brave. She came so close to snuffing her life out before I could claim her.

Perhaps after another round with the dragon tail, she will have atoned.

"The one who shot Stephanos?" I ask as if I'm not aware of the facts.

"Yeah."

"Do you know who she was?"

"Some hooker Stephanos did dirty," Spiro says. "That's what I heard. Johnson took a bullet and went back to his people in Chicago."

"And what about Bruno?" I ask after Stephanos' right-hand man.

"Bruno's loyal," Spiro says, and the rest of the gang nods. They're calmer now, warming up to me. With every passing moment, Uzi lets the gun muzzle bow another inch.

"I need to speak to Stephanos," I say

Uzi jerks his gun back up.

After a glance around the room, Spiro answers. "We haven't seen him in ten or twelve weeks."

"So long? Who's paying you?"

"We've got jobs."

"I know you are busy," I say, allowing them to keep their respect. A quick perusal of the video footage showed them waiting around, eating pizza rolls Spiro bought at the dollar store and cooked in the restaurant microwave. There was some talk of moving equipment left unguarded on the docks, but when Spiro looked into it, the equipment was already gone. "I am prepared to pay you for your time. There's a briefcase there on the front stoop. Locked, but the code is today's date."

Spiro jerks his head at Joe, and the big man lumbers off. Clouds of dust billow up when he opens the door. After looking left and right, he brings the briefcase inside.

"Don't open it," Uzi says. His voice is higher than you'd expect from a grown man. "Could be a bomb."

"Then he'd blow himself up too, dumbass," Spiro says. "Today's date, you say?"

At my nod, Spiro enters the code. The case opens slowly, and the men freeze. You'd think I had handed them a bomb, not a case full of unmarked bills.

"What the fuck is this?" Spiro snarls.

"This was half the take Stephanos advanced me for the wedding. You can split it among yourselves."

Joe scratches his chin again. "What's the catch?"

"I require the rest of the payment. I never received it. I need to contact Stephanos, and to do that, I need your help."

"No," Bruiser blurts, but Spiro elbows him in the chest.

"Shut up." Spiro unpacks a stack of bills and runs his thumb along the edges, counting. "If we connect you with Stephanos, what's in it for us?"

"Another case of unmarked bills."

"This is fucking bullshit," Bruiser mutters, his beady eyes darting to the exits. "Uzi, waste him."

Uzi's staring at the money.

"Fuck this," Bruiser says. "I'll do it myself." He raises his weapon and stares in horror at the knife protruding from his hand. He stands there, blinking at it until the pain rushes in.

"Fuck! My hand!" He waves his hand around, spattering everyone with blood.

"Shut up," Spiro rushes to close the briefcase and protect the money. "Joe—"

Joe steps forward and cold-cocks Bruiser. Bruiser collapses to the dirty floor. With a gush of blood, the knife slides out of his hand, clattering to Joe's feet.

Everyone freezes.

Slowly, Joe reaches down and picks up my knife. He shuffles forward and offers it carefully to me. "I never liked him," he says about poor Bruiser, who is still groaning on the floor.

I accept my knife back with a nod, and the tension in the room goes down a notch.

Spiro hugs the briefcase. "We'll talk to him," he says with a nod at Bruiser. "Explain things."

"There's a burner phone underneath the money," I continue as if we hadn't been interrupted. "I'll call you in two days."

"And if we don't deliver?" Spiro asks, still wary. I can feel the men's eyes crawling over me, trying to figure out where I hide my knives. Wondering how many I have secured away and how quickly I could draw and throw them.

I shrug. "You can keep the cash. I'll find another way. But I plan to stick around this town, and I'm generous to my friends." I give them a big, friendly smile. For some reason, it doesn't seem to reassure them at all. "And it might be nice to be my friends. Don't you agree?"

12

Victor

"He's a fucking maniac. I vote we take the money and blow." This is from Kill Zone. He paces back and forth, waving his hands. "Did you see him smile? My cousin told me he smiled like that when he killed the bean counter at the wedding. Just bam. Dead."

Uzi sits in a corner, cradling his gun like a teddy bear.

Bruiser is nowhere to be seen.

Spiro has the briefcase splayed open on a table, counting stacks. "He could've killed Bruiser. And he didn't."

"He could've killed us all," mutters Joe from his guard post at the door.

I lean back in my chair, watching the blurry shapes of the men on screen. The lagging feed makes them look like puppets, moving jerkily around the room. The visual is poor, but the audio comes through crisp and clear.

"It's all here." Spiro sags into a seat. "Half the advance Stephanos gave him. He wasn't lying."

That gives them all pause. Stacks of cash speak louder than words.

I mute the feed and watch them deliberate. They are on the spectrum between fear and awe, with a little curiosity mixed in. A few of them might cut their losses, take their share of the cash, and leave town. But my bet is that a core group will remain. Their leader, Spiro, has an aging mother in the area, which would make him reluctant to move. He can contact Stephanos. And if he carries the briefcase anywhere, I'll be able to track it.

It's just one tendril, one silken thread I've woven to make my spider's web. In time, I will have Stephanos trapped where I want him. Not today. But soon.

In the meantime, I have sweeter company to keep.

To my right, a smaller screen shows the small room and king bed where I left Lula. The doctor reported that she remained asleep all this time. Her eyes are still closed, but she's more restless, her fingers and toes twitching. I rise and leave the computer room and its monitors. I only have a few minutes to get ready.

My beautiful prisoner is about to wake.

Lula

I blink my eyes open, feeling like an elephant is sitting on me. A heavy blanket is on my lower half, and when I shove it off, I'm able to breathe, but my limbs are still heavy with the languor that comes from a long, uninterrupted sleep. I'm in a big, four-poster bed in a plain, dimly lit room.

There's no way to tell what time it is. My prison isn't the worst hellhole I can imagine, but the lack of clocks or sunlight is driving me mad. In this stifling, windowless space, with no markers of night or day, I'm lost to the world. Adrift in a timeless space with no direction to tell me up from down.

The only constant is my body, my nakedness. And Victor. I hate how my thoughts go to him immediately and constantly. I hate even more how my body revs up at the thought of him.

I could spend a few minutes lying here imagining shooting him properly. His eyebrows are darker than his silver and gold hair, a honey color. A bullet between them would kill him instantly. But then I'd feel the tangle of emotions when I watched the light drain out of his ice-blue eyes.

Suddenly, the bed is too soft and confining for me to stay in a second longer. I stretch and metal clinks. My right wrist is handcuffed to the headboard, but other than that, I'm free.

I'm free!

I swing myself out of bed and brace against the heavy wooden post. Gritting my teeth, I pull my hand against the steel circle of the handcuff. With the right amount of joint-screaming pressure, I pop my thumb out of its socket and wrench it through. Fire blazes up my poor thumb, and I have to swallow my scream, but with my thumb out, my fingers follow easily. Shuddering, sweating, and panting with the pain, I clutch my throbbing hand to my chest and head for the door.

It's unlocked. I stop breathing and turn the knob slowly so as not to make any sound. The space beyond the bedroom is a smaller version of Victor's penthouse. There's a kitchen with a giant quartz-topped island with four black leather-topped bar stools pushed under it. The rest of the area is bare, with a thick plush rug and a single, deep black leather armchair. Doors line the walls, thick and utilitarian. Probably locked. One of them might lead back to the large room where Victor's been holding me. Even if escape lay that way, I wouldn't be able to bring myself to enter the dungeon-like space again.

The first door I open leads to a small bathroom. My bladder screams at me, but I ignore it. Next door, locked. The next, by the kitchen, opens to a dark hallway. I'm through it in a flash, racing down. It's dark, and I pat the walls with my good hand, finding door after door, each one locked.

He comes out of the shadows, his silver-gold hair lighting up the dark. "Lula."

I scream, and he grabs me, tugging me back the way I came. Maybe back to the dungeon—

I kick, and he grunts, then lifts me. I'm a wild thing, thrashing and flailing. I'll do anything to escape him. I can't go back to the dungeon; I just can't—

He drags me down to the rug, his weight falling on me. A few feet away, the open door to the hallway swings shut. I feel the final click, like a guillotine blade slicing down, severing all hope.

"No," I growl.

"Lula," he murmurs in my ear. "You can't have thought it'd be this easy."

I jerk away, but he holds me fast. When I try to free my arms, the move hits my dislocated thumb, and my body seizes with the pain.

I cry out, and he rolls me to my back, pressing me into the floor with his hips heavy on mine.

"Oh, krasiva, what have you done to yourself?" He pins me and reaches for my hand.

I try to wrestle him one-handed, breathlessly pleading, but he immobilizes me.

"Shhhh, precious one. I'm not going to hurt you." He shifts his weight so he's not crushing me.

Whimpering, I let him take my hand and study it.

"Correction. This will hurt for a moment." He searches my eyes until I nod and pops my thumb back into place. My whole body seizes, screaming, and then I slump, panting.

He bundles me in his lap, and I settle there, draped against his chest, while the sweat dries on my back, and my body gets used to the empty feeling where the pain used to be. The fight's gone out of me. . . for now.

After a few minutes, my breathing matches his.

"I need to use the bathroom," I tell him quietly. He rises effortlessly, still holding me, and carries me to the bathroom. For a moment, I'm afraid he'll stay with me in the small space, but he sets me down, waits until I'm no longer wobbling on my feet, and, with a brisk kiss on my forehead, leaves me. I sink down onto the toilet, feeling pathetically grateful.

I spend long moments in the bathroom, finger-combing my hair and scrubbing my face with one hand, scolding myself the whole time. *He's the enemy. He's the worst.*

But when I warily exit the bathroom, I can't help searching for him. And when I see him, barefoot and broad-shouldered, standing in the kitchen area, my heart flutters.

"Hello, beautiful." His eyes crinkle as he smiles. Behind the island, tending to something on the stove, he's the picture of domestic bliss. A boyfriend welcoming me home.

I've never had a boyfriend. If I had, he wouldn't be model-pretty like Victor. A sense of satisfaction hums through me, pleasure that this beautiful creature is, for the moment, mine.

Which is stupid. I'm his prisoner. I have to remember that, and resist.

The scent of sautéed onions hits me, and my stomach cramps.

Victor signals me forward. I halt at his stupid hand gesture, but he doesn't seem to notice as he's too busy plating something mouthwatering and sliding it across the island to a place setting. "You must be hungry."

An omelet. He's made me an omelet sprinkled with finely cut chives. And it looks like something out of a cooking magazine, damn him.

I cross the space to him, feeling the pull toward him deep in my belly.

In this mundane setting, I feel my nakedness even more. Again, I'm naked while he's clothed, and the powerful contrast makes my core throb. When I slide onto the stool, the cool leather makes goosebumps break out over my body.

"Cold?" he asks, and I nod.

He unbuttons his black shirt and comes around the island to help me into it. It's huge on me, draping over my thighs like a shirt dress. He has to roll up the sleeves so I can eat. My heart slams happily in the cage of my ribs as he dresses me. He purses his plush lips and fiddles with the fabric, his nimble fingers tucking and straightening the black silk.

And when he returns to the stove, leaving me sitting there in the soft shirt that smells of him and still retains his body heat, I want to cry.

I stare at the shirt buttons. I get it now. This is how he's going to break me. Not with cruelty. With kindness.

Shirtless, Victor finishes cooking his own meal. The muscles in his back and shoulders ripple with each lazy movement. "You're not eating," he says with a frown, and my heart leaps. Will he punish me? Drag me back to the cage?

I glance at the heavy door that leads to the hallway. If only I had made it out.

"Lula. You must eat."

"Or what?" I ask, my stomach roiling. "You'll hurt me?"

He drops his elbows to the white quartz on either side of his plate and leans in. "No. I won't hurt you again unless you beg me."

I hiss in a breath. The scent of the food is making me so weak I might fall off the stool, but every cell in me wants to fight. "Are you insane?"

"Probably." He picks up his fork and digs into his eggs. "The official diagnosis is antisocial personality disorder."

"I'm not going to beg you."

He smiles at his plate.

"I'm still going to fight you," I say, testing the words.

Okay, he signals. "I wouldn't have it any other way."

I dig into my omelet.

It's fucking delicious.

Victor finishes his food before I do. I take my time, savoring each buttery bite, hoping if I draw out this meal, I'll be able to put off whatever happens next.

He watches me with a half smile as if he knows what I'm doing but finds it amusing.

"How long did I sleep?" I ask, less hoping he'll tell me and more to stretch meal time.

"Long enough. I would've stayed with you, but I had business."

I use my fork to cut a piece of omelet into a perfect golden square. "What sort of business?"

"Tracking down Stephanos." He says it calmly, as if he didn't just drop a live grenade into the conversation.

"Why?"

"He owes me. The last payment for my last job."

"David," I say, and he nods.

"He paid the first half promptly. But before I could collect the second half, I was incapacitated."

Because I shot him. "That's a shame," I say with a straight face.

"Indeed." He clears his plate and washes it right away. It would take me a few seconds to rush around the island to jab my fork into his kidney. But I doubt he's distracted enough to let me. Besides, the pale, muscled expanse of his back is so pretty. And I want to keep eating.

"Stephanos has gone to ground," Victor tells me as he cleans up the cooking area.

"I know." I grind my teeth.

"But I found several members of his gang and spoke to them today. One way or another, they will lead me to him."

When Victor turns from the sink, I'm gripping the fork like a weapon.

"Lula, breathe."

"What will you do when you find him?"

"Retrieve what is owed to me. One way or another."

"Will you kill him?"

"Do you want me to?" He looks me dead in the eye. It's a genuine question.

"No. I can't afford to hire you. Left my wallet in my other pants."

His expression doesn't change at my little joke. Which is fine. I don't feel like laughing, either.

My appetite is gone, but I poke at my food, unwilling for the meal to be over. "How many people have you killed?"

Victor tilts his head as if he's doing mental math. "Men and women?"

I have a horrifying thought. "Do you kill children?" There's a metallic taste in my mouth.

"No. No one under the age of twenty-two. There are rarely contracts on children unless they are heirs."

I feel the tiniest bit of relief. The psychopath has standards.

He's still a monster, I scold myself. I don't want to think about this dark world that Victor lives in, but I can't help myself. "What you told me last night. The story of the little boy. Was any of it true?"

"There are no lies between us." He leans over the island, and that slight movement is enough to send his winter-fresh scent wafting my way.

"Why?"

"You know why."

I want to protest, but he's staring at me so intently, gaze scalpel-sharp enough to dissect me, that I have to look away.

"Everything I told you was true. My mother slept with men for money. She did her best to survive. A butcher took us in and gave us food and a place to stay. In return, my mother did whatever he wanted, and I worked for him in the shop. He taught me everything I know." He's leaning into the island counter, gripping the edge. It looks casual, but his fingers tighten until they're almost as white as the quartz. "One night, he hit my mother, and I killed him. I used his favorite knife to cut him into pieces. A graduation of sorts."

I swallow. "How old were you?"

"Thirteen."

I blink rapidly. My heart bleeds for the young, tow-headed boy. "And your mother?"

"Dead. I had to run, you see, and she had to hide. She found another man, but he hit her, and it was fatal. I killed him, too."

"My god."

"There is no god." He stalks around the island to stand over me. The wound in his stomach is on display, the bullet puncture a half-healed pink. His head is bowed and shadows lie in the hollows under his cheekbones. "Are you finished?"

Yes, please, let's change the subject. I lean back to let him take my plate and invite a new danger. My skin prickles as he reaches over me. In this setting, it's easy to imagine him as a friend or a lover. I'm not a hugger, but all that beautiful muscle, godlike in its perfection? I want to draw him close under the pretense of comfort. Lay my head on his pecs. Slide my hands up his strong back. There's an ache deep in my gut, one that will only dissolve if I touch him. He's so close I'd only have to move an inch...

I swallow and deliberately angle myself away from him.

I can sense him silently laughing as he carries my plate away.

"Is this some sort of plan to make me care about you?" I ask sourly. "To make me empathize with you so I feel like we're on the same side?"

"We are on the same side."

He's at the sink again, his back to me, but I shake my head. "I mean some sort of psychological conditioning."

"Stockholm syndrome?"

"Yes. Except Stockholm syndrome was developed by a cop-sympathizing psychologist to discredit a witness's testimony. A woman's testimony. It's more likely she felt real empathy for her captors."

"You are the expert." A smile hides behind his dry tone.

"Shut up."

He finishes the dishes and returns to me. I slide off the stool, not wanting to act too nervous but needing something physical between us. My hands fist at my side, and I will myself not to run. Not to look towards the dungeon door.

"What now?" I finally ask to keep from screaming.

"More training." Before I can throw myself in the opposite direction, he says, "Not that sort." He flicks his fingers, and where they were once empty, they now hold a shining blade. "I'm going to teach you how to throw a knife."

13

Victor

HER DARK BROWS KNIT TOGETHER. "Are you serious?"

"Trade you." I offer her the knife handle first. It's one of my favorites, a fixed-blade combat knife, both handle and blade a rain cloud gray.

She stares at it. "Is this for real?

"A trade." I point to her right hand and signal her to *Come.* "The fork, Lula."

She sets the fork on the island and reaches for the knife, every movement broadcasting that she doesn't believe this is happening and expecting a bait and switch.

It will take time, but eventually, she will realize I am honest with her and worthy of her trust.

A sign escapes her when she palms the knife handle. Her entire stance relaxes. This woman was born to hold a weapon.

"You're really going to teach me?"

"Yes."

"And if I attack you?"

I shrug. "You'll learn faster." I wait for her to make a decision. If she rushes me, I can overpower her. If she runs, it might be difficult to catch her. Untrained, she's more of a danger to herself than she is to me.

"What if I don't want to learn?"

"There are other ways to pass the time."

She clicks her tongue, and I know I have her. She wants to know what happens next. In a world filled with many dull moments and even duller people, curiosity is our greatest weakness.

Come, I gesture to her. "The training area is this way."

"Like this?" She gestures to her bare legs. She looks fantastic in my shirt, the tails just covering her soft backside and the tops of her thighs.

"I'll give you more to wear if you are good."

She scoffs and tosses her hair over her shoulder.

I lead her to the door with the hallway, and her breath catches. The hall is long and dim, lined with locked doors. I can sense her calculating her chances of escape.

"I thought you'd take me back to the dungeon."

"No more dungeon." I underscore this with a *No* signal. "You've earned a reward. New living quarters." I spread my hands. "And a live-in chef."

Her eyes narrow. She's gripping the knife hard enough to whiten her knuckles.

I jerk up my chin. "Toss it at me." *Come*, my fingers say.

She looks startled. I spread my arms wider, presenting a bigger target. Her gaze lingers on the ridges and contour of my chest, and her breath comes faster. Imagining fucking or killing me?

Probably both. She's the only person in the world who wants to please and hurt me in equal measure.

I feel the same about her.

The minute stretches on. "Let me see how you throw."

She grips the knife tighter. She doesn't want to lose it.

"We're not sparring?"

"I'd rather you not risk fighting in hand-to-hand combat."

"Because I'm a woman?"

"There are advantages to being smaller and lighter, but only if you're faster."

She smirks. "I'm only fast when I'm eating pastries."

I'm about to command her again when her arm snaps back, and she whips the knife in my direction.

I catch it easily. It was a sloppy throw, angling towards the floor. With my right hand, I toss it up and down, catching it each time. With my free hand, I reach out to a panel on the wall and punch a few buttons. At the end of a hall, a ceiling panel retracts, and a large wooden target lowers. I pace closer and point to where I want her to stand. After a pause, she follows and obeys.

"Stand here. Like this." I put her through her paces, running my hands down her legs so she shifts into the proper stance, cupping her hips and angling them. Pulling back her hair and pressing a kiss to her shoulder. She shudders but gives me a glare that makes me glad I have the knife.

Then I stand behind her, pressed to her back as I move her arm with mine to mimic the proper throwing technique. With her naked, there's nothing between her curvy ass and my groin but the thin fabric of my slacks. The more we move together, the more unsteady her breath. She tries to hide it, but I know her. Every rise and fall of her glorious breasts. The furrow in her forehead as she tries to master the movement.

My cock is hard and throbbing, poking into her lower back. I take a moment to push against her, burying my face in her hair to inhale her scent.

She waits, tense, for me to breathe in my full.

“Why are you doing this?”

“Killing with a gun is easy but killing with a knife?” I flip the dagger so the handle is at my lips, and the blade digs into my palm. “It is much more… satisfying.”

She shakes her head slightly, making her hair fall against my shoulder. “Psycho.”

“No, that’s like this.” I mime the overhand strike Norman Bates used.

“Ha. Ha.”

I catch her hand and press the knife into it, continuing my instruction. “Now.” I move her arm until she’s loose and limber, then coach her through a throw. “All the way through. As if you’re slashing someone.” The knife smacks the target, but the tip doesn’t catch, so it clatters to the floor.

“Again.” I trace a circle with my pointer finger, then pat her ass until she heads down the hall to retrieve the weapon. The sight of her swaying away from me has my groin tightening. Her bare body is a thing of beauty, but the bruises from her last session have faded. I’ll have to do something about that later.

I make her throw again and again, driving through the motion until her right arm falters. Then I teach her a left-handed throw. Her chest is heaving, her golden skin slick from exertion.

At last, the knife thunks into the wood, right through a seam. I go to fetch it and touch the tip protruding from the other side. “It went through. Well done, Lula.”

She comes to examine it herself. She's breathing hard but glowing, her eyes lit with a triumphant light.

"I killed it."

"You did." I give her the *Good girl* signal, and she doesn't frown at my fingers like she usually does.

She works to wrench the knife out, and as she does, I slip behind her, running my palm down her belly as I kiss her shoulder. "You did well." I let my hand delve between her thighs, cupping her heat. "You get a reward."

It only takes a few minutes to work her up with my fingers. I know just where to rub and press and tug. As her muscles tighten, I work a finger into her backside, letting her anus clench on my fingertip. Soon, I'll introduce her to a plug. She'll only be allowed to cum with something filling her rear until she associates anal with pleasure.

I worm my finger in deeper. She twists in my arms but ultimately settles, accepting the intrusion along with the clitoral stimulation. In no time, she's gasping and shaking through her climax. I keep stroking her, stoking the pleasure higher, forcing her through another and another.

Finally, I take my hand away. She slumps forward, and all her weight falls into my arms, pulling me off balance. It's only for a second, but it's enough. Her feet find the ground, and she snaps up, her elbow coming toward my face. I turn at the last second and grapple with her, drawing her arm behind her, but she's determined and falls to her knees. I fall with her, but she has enough of an advantage to scramble away from me. She looks feral on all fours, hair falling wild around her snarling face. She still has the knife.

I smile and crouch and signal her to *Come.*

She lunges, knife first, and I hit her wrist hard enough to make her drop it. From there, it's easy to tug her shirt down and restrict her movements. She shucks it off and lets it drop, leaving her naked, which is fine by me.

I stalk towards her, and she turns to run, trying every locked door. Eventually, I corral her back into the living area. She races to the kitchen, probably to look for another weapon, and I lunge, using the advantage of my height and weight to bring her to the ground, face down on the rug, with her arms wrenched backward into my hold.

She yells into the rug, shaking with the force of it.

I lean down and murmur into her dark hair. "To the victor go the spoils."

That earns me another shout of rage. I ease off her, and she pushes up, attacking me again with her nails stretched toward my eyes.

This time, I catch her wrists and slam her onto her back, pinning her wrists to either side of her head. With my weight half on her, I can keep her immobilized for hours or as long as it takes for her to regain some control of herself.

Slowly, the rage bleeds out of her dark eyes.

"Good work. You almost cut me. If we spar to first blood, that would be a win."

She bares her teeth at me. "I want more than first blood."

"We'll have to practice then. I'll reward you when you win. But since you lost. . ." I ease off and flip her over. She lands face down over my lap. I don't have cuffs at hand, but it's a pleasure to restrain her and watch her bottom and thigh muscles ripple as she struggles. I slap her ass, letting my broad palm catch as much of her rear as I can. She yelps, and I continue punishing her, hard and fast, while her shoulders and hips rock, and she tries to wriggle away. I drape a leg over hers, pinning them down. I spank her ass red until her hips are surging up and down, seeking stimulation.

I've trained her to crave pain. I raise a knee under her, letting her rub against my leg until she's close, then flip her to her back with a hand at her throat. "Little savage. This isn't for you."

I swat at her hands and use my knees to spread her legs. After a minute of wrestling, I pin her again and open my pants. I have her where I want her: her arms overhead and breasts lifted, her legs wide, and my cock nudging her folds. "I won. Now I get my reward."

~

LULA

VICTOR'S huge body blankets me, pressing me to the rug. My bottom is hot and swollen from my spanking, my core pulsing with need. His cock is at my entrance, and I'm wet enough for him to slide right in. But as soon as he tells me he's won, I start fighting again.

I wriggle and try to ram him in the gut, aiming for the tender spot on his abdomen where my bullet went in. His jaw tightens—he's so beautiful when he's angry—and he drapes more of his weight on me, pinning me down.

I force him to tighten his grip until he's hurting me. This isn't some sweet lover's tryst. Sure, he cooked me breakfast and introduced me to his favorite pastime, but we're not sweethearts tangling on the floor, too overcome with lust to make it to the bedroom. He is my enemy, and I am his.

I cannot forget that. No matter how many orgasms he gives me.

His cock punches into me. My core clenches on that first blunt inch. He's so big it always takes a few minutes to adjust to him. Today, he's not giving me time.

"Let me in." He emphasizes each word with a kick of his hips. He's merciless in his invasion, and despite myself, my body softens and swallows him up. And, fates help me, it feels so damn good.

I widen my legs and arch off the floor. He lessens the amount of weight on my smaller frame. "That's it. Good girl."

"Fuck you."

"With pleasure." He rocks into me, and warmth rolls up my torso, blooming in my brain. He moves slowly, and I savor every drag of his long and thick rod. Lights spark behind my eyes.

All too soon, his thrusts turn savage. He clasps my hands and drives into me, holding me captive to his plundering. It's too much. I want more.

I'm not fighting him anymore. My knees are open wide, and I let myself wrap my legs above his taut buttocks in an attempt to keep up with his punishing rhythm. His face is frozen in an intent grimace, the pale marble of his sculpted arms and chest glistening with sweat. He shifts to his knees, putting his giant hands under my bottom and jackhammering deeper. The head of his cock battering at my womb. My orgasms blow up like a bomb. Again and again, until I lose count of the detonations.

Victor hoists me up and carries me to the armchair, where he flips me face down onto the seat cushion so he can fuck me from behind. I grip the leather until it's slippery with my sweat. With Victor wedged inside me, my knees don't quite meet the floor, but it doesn't matter. He doesn't stop slamming into me, driving me forward until I'm clawing at the seat back for purchase. He draws my head back by my hair. Every time he tugs, I clench around him. Somehow I cum again this way, my head tipped back and mouth open, trying to drag oxygen into my lungs.

He flips me again and stands, holding me in his arms. I clutch his shoulders, and he grabs my hips, forcing me down on his cock again. Slowly, he impales me, letting gravity drag me down. At this angle, he's so deep that I feel him in the back of my throat. When he works my hips for me, sliding me up and down, I stare down at the angry red inches disappearing inside me.

My legs vibrate in one continuous, nonstop climax.

And then we're in his bedroom, and he's letting me sink into the plush mattress before propping my legs over his shoulders and powering into me.

He's still impossibly hard. I cannot believe his stamina.

Times like these, I think I should've shot him in the dick. But it'd be a crime to deprive the world of the most perfect penis in existence.

And just as I'm fantasizing about killing him again, he slides a hand up my backside and presses a finger into my ass. I come hard, feeling him everywhere, and he finally follows me over. I clench down on his cock, loving the way he surges inside me.

We lie on our sides for a moment, panting. I need a nap, and I'm going to be sore when I wake up. Victor fucks like he lives—with joyful violence.

"You like my finger in your ass?" He twists his digit deeper.

"No," I say, just as a mini-tremor runs through me.

"Liar." He probes me mercilessly. Just when I've stretched around his single finger, he adds another.

Meanwhile, his cock is growing harder inside me. As it

swells, it adds pressure against the fragile wall between it and his fingers.

"Fuck me," I moan.

"As you wish." He removes his fingers from my ass and swings into the cradle of my hips.

"Again?"

"You can take it."

I mutter something unintelligible. At least now we're in bed. I watch him through half-closed eyes, letting him use my body to sate himself. I'm a tiny sailboat rocking on an endless ocean.

A warm cloth to my sex snaps me awake.

"Lula, my Lula." He's cleaning me, kissing me. Then he turns his head and sweeps his tongue up my cheek, licking the tears off my face. I bare my teeth at him half-heartedly, and he laughs. "You want to mark me, my vicious beauty?" He settles my hand at the wound on his gut. "You already have."

His skin is smooth under my palm. This is the moment. I could dig my fingers in, break the still-fragile scar tissue, and draw his blood. Instead, I simply rest my hand over the wound, savoring the feel of him. I've never liked cuddling, but Victor is huge and powerful, and the basest part of me registers him as safe. He'd never allow anyone to hurt me. He'd reserve that right for himself.

Sleep is rising to claim me. I try to fend it off, muttering, "I should've aimed for the heart." I slide my hand up to his left pectoral. He presses his own hand on top of mine, forcing me to feel his heartbeat thundering in time with mine.

"You may not have aimed for it, but you hit it all the same."

LULA

IT'S dark in the bedroom when Victor wakes me, rolling me to my side so he can raise my thigh and slide into me.

"You're nuts," I mutter into the pillow. I don't know what time it is, but it feels like the middle of the night. I half doze as he uses my body, only waking when he grunts in satisfaction and folds me into him, kissing the top of my head. I settle in his arms, trying to decide whether the wetness between my legs is his fresh cum or my own arousal.

"Finished?"

"For now." He kisses my forehead. "Sleep. You need it. I'll wake you when it's time to eat."

"I want pancakes." I let sleep claim me again.

At our next meal, he makes me pancakes and lets me wear his shirt the whole time. When I'm full, he pulls me into the hall where he's set up a wooden dummy and teaches me to slash and cut with a knife. "I'd prefer you never need to fight in close combat. But better to be prepared."

He has me throw knives at a target until my arms are tired and rewards me with a shower and an easy, slow fuck against the tiled walls. Then he uses a straight razor to shave me. Once we're clean and dry, he props me on all fours in the bed next to a black towel with a tube of lube and a small black plug on top of it.

He strokes my bottom. "Are you going to fight me?"

"I don't know." I glare at him over my shoulder. "Are you gonna put that in my ass?"

"Would you prefer to do it yourself?"

"What do you think?" I let him plant a hand between my shoulder blades and push me down so my cheek is flush with the bedspread, my ass high in the air.

"Push out," he orders and probes me with lube-coated fingers before replacing them with the plug. I blow out a breath at the alien feeling, but it's not so bad. What's worse is how he uses his free hand to play with my pussy, and how quickly I grow wet for him.

"Now what?"

"Now a reward." He twists his fingers into my pussy, finds the rough wall above my entrance, and rubs it. "Do you want me to tie you down?" But I'm already rocking into his hand, the plug adding another dark dimension to my climax.

Much later, he makes me what I think of as a late lunch—thick steaks cooked to perfection. He sits on a bar stool next to me and feeds me bite by bite. And I let him because the meat is too amazing to refuse. Melt-in-the-mouth buttery.

It's super weird sitting on a stool with a plug in my ass. But it's not that bad. At least I'm not bound with clamps on my nipples.

It's the little things.

He pours me a glass of wine, a Châteauneuf-du-Pape that's beyond compare to my cheap merlots. I lounge in the armchair, tipped onto one hip so I don't jar the plug in my rear, savoring the smooth but complex red while he does the dishes. Just another episode of Life with a Hitman: Domestic Edition.

It's been a while—at least a week or two—since I've had anything alcoholic to drink, so a few sips go to my head.

"You'll be happy to know I made contact with men who can find Stephanos," Victor tells me, speaking over his shoulder from his spot at the sink.

"You did?"

"Yes. They have not yet led me to him, but they will."

I stare at the ripples in my wine. Having this conversation with Victor is weird. I'm used to thinking of him as an enemy united with Stephanos.

"I asked them who the mole is."

"Did they tell you?"

"No, but I will tell you when I find out." He dries another dish. "Your cousin is looking for you."

"Of course he is." I can imagine my cousin now, standing with arms braced on his desk, barking orders to his men, and only taking breaks to comfort Leah.

"He's intensified the search. Offering a reward for any proof of life."

"Can I get word to him?"

"What would you say?"

That shuts me up. What could I say that Victor would allow? "Wanted: tall blond hitman. Likes to torture people. If spotted. . ." I hesitate.

"Shoot to kill?" Victor dries his hands on a dish towel hanging neatly on the oven handle. The dish towel is a creamy white, decorated with little yellow ducks because why not?

"Maim," I say. I don't sound certain. Victor prowls over, holding the wine bottle. He tops me off, then sets the bottle down and scoops me up, only to sit with me in his lap. And I let him. I'm more worried about spilling the wine.

I settle into his arms like we're a couple decompressing after a long day's work. A half-naked couple, him only wearing soft slacks and me in nothing—no bra, no panties —but his shirt. And a butt plug.

For a while, Victor does nothing but stroke my back and watch me sip my wine.

Maybe I'm tipsy, but this is nice. The plug is still annoying, but its presence makes my pussy wet.

"Do you like it?" He tips his head towards the glass.

"It's good." It's my turn to turn to him and hold the glass to give him a sip. Which might be a mistake because it leaves his hands free to roam. He trails his fingers over my hip and into the cleft of my bottom, finding the flat end of the plug. He does nothing more than tap it, but I feel the vibration deep in my core.

He just watches me, noting every twitch of my facial muscles, every catch in my breathing.

After a time, he leans in, stirring my hair with a silky whisper. "Do you like your plug?"

I won't dignify that with a response. He doesn't need one. His roaming hand finds my bare pussy and the dampness there.

"If you don't tell me, I'll have to check." He's thorough, too, his fingers dancing from clit to plug and back again. My mind goes blank from the wine, from his touch.

He only stops to pour me more wine. Only a quarter of the bottle left.

"How does this end?" I ask the open air.

He's drawn down my shirt to play with my breasts, and he brushes his lips across the top of my shoulder.

"Victor," I call his name to catch his attention. "Will you ever let me go?"

"You know the answer to that." His long fingers trail over my curves, dipping between them. His callouses catch on my nipples, and my stomach muscles tighten. "We belong together."

I scoff.

"Can you imagine your life without me?" I open my mouth, and he pinches my nipple in anticipation. "No lies."

"I'm a lawyer. I twist the truth for a living."

"Then let this be the time and place you tell the truth. Not only to me but to yourself." He loosens his grip on my nipple, rolling it between his fingers instead. "If I disappeared tomorrow, would you miss me?"

I imagine it. The empty rooms, the unlocked doors. I'd get my escape, but... "I'd be pissed."

"Would you hunt me down?" He sounds amused, as if predator and prey is a game we play.

Maybe it is.

"Yes."

"And when you caught me, would you kill me?"

I try to imagine my life before Victor. Nothing but long hours of work for La Famiglia. Nights I spent alone with my resentment and my red wine. Bad wine compared to the heady ambrosia I'm drinking now. "No."

"So you would miss me. Or perhaps only the orgasms I give you?"

"I crave them," I finally admit. "I crave you."

"It's not a weakness to need another person."

I want to scoff again, to roll my eyes. He's wrong. Needing someone is the greatest weakness of all. Instead, I challenge him like the lawyer I am. "Who do you need?"

"You."

I don't want to believe him. But he takes my wine, drinks it down in one deep swallow, and takes me back to bed to prove how much one part of his anatomy needs me. Several orgasms later, I'm back to drifting off in his arms, enveloped in his wintry scent. I'm not thinking of how I could incapacitate him and escape. I'm thinking of steaks and massages and sessions on the cross. Secrets whispered in the middle of the night.

Being the one person in the world this dangerous man needs? Fate, save me from this exquisite hell. I do not want to give it up.

14

L*ula*

SEVEN MEALS, five bottles of wine, three training sessions with the knife, and many, many fucks later, he has me tied up, standing in the middle of the room. My arms are cuffed over my head, and there's a blindfold over my face. I have a spreader bar between my legs, a plug in my ass, a gag in my mouth, and a diabolical shield over my clit that vibrates at odd intervals.

He places a plush sphere into my hand. "Squeeze." I do, and the ball squeaks like a dog toy.

"Squeeze this three times, and I'll stop." He waits for me to nod, then adds the finishing touch of plugs in my ears.

When he's done, I can't see, and I can't hear. I flex my free hand in the bindings, reaching for something. Proof of the world beyond this dark, silent place.

His hand at my hip steadies me, and I know he's chosen something particularly wicked to begin with.

A line of fire blazes across both globes of my ass.

My hand clenches, but I don't squeeze the toy.

Another stripe across my sit spots. A third below that.

I strain, but I can't hear anything. Not that it'd be a mercy to hear the implement whistling through the air or cracking on my flesh, but at least it would be something to focus on other than the throbbing stripes on my buttocks and the backs of my thighs.

Another stroke and subsequent sting. A fifth slanting over the rest. My rear is a fiery mass, each caned line pulsing in echoing waves.

I dangle, half dancing in my high heels, twisting this way and that. The flogger comes to bite my breasts, and I drop the ball.

Sweat rolls down my chest, beading between my breasts. I can smell the animal scent of me.

And I can smell the cool winter wind of Victor.

He leans into me, returning the ball to my hand. I squeeze it once to prove that I'm still with him.

His lips caress mine. Cool mint, a bite of pine. I sigh.

Then the nipple clamps come. And more flogging on my back. I lean from side to side, shifting my weight in the small increments I'm allowed by the spreader bar and the bindings on my wrists. I turn my head, but the blindfold lets in no light, no shapes, and the earplugs allow no sound.

I can only feel.

A crop on my pussy.

A paddle on my ass.

A tightening of the nipple clamps so they pinch with a sharper bite.

Victor's fingers trail over the marks he made, and I can only imagine his satisfied expression.

The shield on my clit trembles to life, buzzing in rising surges. I rock to tiptoe, fighting to close my legs and get more stimulation.

Victor strokes my inner thighs, taunting me.

I moan around the gag. The sound is worlds away.

He presses on the shield, giving me the pressure I need. All the agony in my body rushes in fiery rivulets toward the beautiful feeling in my pussy. As my core contracts, the bright red burn turns to gold.

His breath caresses my face, and I can sense him murmuring, "Beautiful. Bellissima. Good girl."

He unplugs my ears and gives me water.

"Had enough?"

I shake my head. The smarting lines on my backside and the sting in my nipples have faded to nothing. The pain is no longer enough to balance the excruciating sweetness of my climax.

I don't know what I have to prove. Why I always want more.

But Victor does, and he answers my unspoken questions. "You need it to hurt. You like to earn it."

"Yes. Give it to me."

"I will, beautiful one. I will."

And he lays into me harder than before. He never replaced the earplugs, so I hear each swish and crack. The strokes come faster, merging from one into the other until I have no time to brace for them. So I surrender to them and welcome the pain. I want it. I need it. It burns like a cleansing fire, and I'm caught in the crucible and reborn.

A hand at my hip steadies me again. Slowly, Victor draws out the plug in my ass and pumps it back in. At first, I tense, but there's no fighting it. My body relaxes, accepting the strange sensation. When he pulls it out all the way, I clench, seeking the dark stimulation.

I don't have long to miss it. He sets his cock at my gaping hole and presses in. He's slick with lube, but the stretch still burns. Any desire to be filled is replaced by panic at the blunt intrusion.

"Breathe, Lula," he growls. I suck in oxygen, feeling dizzy, and he wedges himself deeper into my ass. His arm snakes around my midriff to press on the buzzing vibrator over my clit.

And I cum, hard and long, my muscles seizing and clamping on his cock.

He curses and mutters something long and intent in his native tongue. Slowly, he eases out of me, giving me a hint of relief before pushing back in. He's gentle, and the device on my clit doesn't block my pussy, so he's free to press his fingers inside me. I clench around them, gripping them like a lifeline as the burn in my bottom flares into something new, something disturbingly like pleasure.

"That's it. Good girl." He pushes another finger into my pussy, his wrist pressing on the vibrator, his dick stretching me impossibly wide.

His free hand comes to my throat.

"Are you going to cum for me, beautiful? With my cock in your ass?"

"Fuck."

"Yes." His dick saws in and out of me. Another few passes and his fingers catch just the right spot inside me, making me shudder through another climax. "I think you like this, Lula." He plucks away the vibrator and replaces it with his palm, roughly scrubbing my swollen bud until I'm thrashing, trying to get away.

I can't get away. I'm strung up like a piece of meat, striped red, and now subject to him fucking me in my last virgin hole. And I like it.

Fates help me, but I love it.

He shoves his fingers, wet from my pussy, into my mouth. I bite down, tasting the sour-sweet of my own cunt. He thrusts into my back channel, making me rise to tiptoes. He's not going to be gentle. Not anymore.

He removes his fingers from my mouth and pulls off a nipple clamp. I cry out, and

I don't know what's more excruciating, the bite of the clamp, the removal, or the final, awful relief.

He waits a while before removing the other one.

"Fucking sadist."

He gives a dark chuckle and power into me, fucking me hard enough that I'll feel it for days.

The blindfold falls away, and I gasp. I'd grown used to the dark. Leave it to Victor to give me what I want and completely ruin it.

He pulls out of my ass, and I hang for a moment, panting. Bereft.

Leave it to Victor to give me what I hate and make me crave it.

"Don't worry, krasiva. I am not done with you."

He uncuffs my ankles from the spreader bar and cuts me down from the overhead bindings. I collapse into his arms. His powerful arms are strong and ready to catch me. His skin is hot and glistening with sweat, and I'm surrounded by his delicious scent.

He carries me to the bed and cleans me up before laying me out for inspection.

More water. A few more kisses.

Then, a hand at my throat, pinning me. Something silver flashes in the corner of my eye, and I startle.

He's holding a knife.

"One more thing," he says as I track the blade's movement. Now that he's trained me to hold one, to throw one, I can spot the expert skill in his elegant fingers. The black handle, the silver tang, the honed edge, it's all a part of him.

He uses the hand that holds the knife to stroke the tendrils of my hair back from my face. "I have waited for this moment since the morning you left me."

The morning I shot him.

He waves the blade in front of my face. I'm pinned by his hand at my throat, limp from the gauntlet of agony and ecstasy he put me through. But I'm still strong enough to fight.

I don't fight. I don't move.

I want to know what happens next.

He sets the knife at my heart. "You marked me. And now I'll mark you."

I hold his gaze. The thin line of frost around the rising darkness. If this is the end, I am not afraid. "Do it."

The first cut is perfect. The sides of my flesh peel away from the sharp edge. Then the blood wells up, darker than I imagined. And it hurts. It hurts like he's cut too deep. Like he's carving his mark on my heart and not just the layer of flesh above.

A second slice, angling towards the first. He's carved a V over my left breast. V for Victor. Proof of his victory over me.

His eyes are fully black now. He doesn't stop but gives me another three strokes to form a second letter. My breath stutters in and out of me, my nerves screaming. But I don't tell him to stop.

I crane my neck to see, but the blood streams in every direction, blotting out what he's carved.

This is the end, yes, but it's also the beginning.

"Lula." He captures my lips, pressing down against me with an insistent hunger. He tips my hips back and slides into my ass again. This time, I can watch him invade me, inch by punishing inch. When he's fully rooted, he presses on my sex, scrubbing the sodden folds until my orgasm blooms and I soften and accept another quarter inch of his cock. My ass is full of him.

My brain is full of warring sensations. I push against his hard, bare chest with arms weakened by the pain over my heart. The smooth marble of his muscles is pink, stained by my blood. I plant bloody handprints all over him—his shoulders, his pecs, his face—until our lips touch, and I taste metal and salt and *us.*

And then he's coming, deep in my ass. Another part of me has ceded to his rule. But I don't care because he cleans me up so carefully and rolls us to a fresh, clean section of the king bed so I can fall asleep in his arms.

I wake to him bandaging me. I still haven't seen what he carved into me, but I can feel it throbbing through my chest like it went all the way to my back. The soreness extends into my left arm.

He pauses, his hand hovering over the white bandage. A shark's smile hovers at the corner of his mouth. He's happy with his work.

He feeds me some pain pills and holds a glass of water to my lips. The pain recedes behind a gauzy curtain.

"Sleep," he orders. "It's still late."

It must be night. I savor this sliver of the outside world he's gifted me. "Late?"

"Yes." Another kiss. In the darkness, he moves beside me, warm and familiar. A partner, a trusted lover, coaxing me back to sleep. "I'll wake you in the morning."

Mornings with Victor, barefoot and shirtless in the kitchen. Eggs. Pancakes. I fall back asleep, smiling.

~

Victor

I've never slept as well as I do with Lula. Even as a boy, I rested in fits and starts, listening to the cacophony of the crime-ridden neighborhood where we could afford to live. Angry voices, slamming doors, back-firing cars and shots fired, I never got used to it. I learned to sleep lightly, to startle awake, warn my mother, and protect her.

But now I rest deeply and fully, my arms full of my captive. My vicious angel.

She makes me feel things, and I'm not used to feeling things. But the small, stunted part of me recognizes that she is the only one who can awaken these emotions. I need her close. She is my soul.

After two REM cycles, I rise reluctantly. I leave Lula sleeping on her back, the bandage over my initials bright in the darkness, and head to the locked drawer in the kitchen that holds the most important of my burner phones.

I wait seven minutes before making the call.

"I'm here," Spiro answers. Over the past few days, I've worked to gain his trust. Now, I'll learn if my efforts paid off.

"Do we have an agreement?"

Spiro pauses. "What's it worth to you?"

"Name your price."

He does, and when I agree to it, he tells me the information I asked for. All of it.

I hang up, heavy with the news I have for Lula.

Our time of reprieve is over. Last night marked a turning point for us. I know she felt it.

Now it's time to learn whether it was the end of the beginning or the beginning of the end.

LULA

I WAKE SLOWLY AND STRETCH, wincing as it pulls the tender skin above my left breast. Victor's left more painkillers beside me and a glass of water. Considerate sadist.

As I have so many mornings, I pad out of the bedroom and find him at the stove, making a meal. Unlike most mornings, I almost smile when I see him clad all in black, his white-blond head in the fridge. His T-shirt shows off the taut muscles and veins of his forearms.

My mouth waters. "Morning."

He signals me to *Come*, and when I do, he sets a bluish smoothie in front of me. I didn't even hear the blender. I taste yogurt and berries.

He watches me drink it, his face a beautiful mask. *Okay?* Another hand signal. He uses them constantly now, especially when he's teaching me how to attack someone with a knife.

"A little sore. Let's go easy on training today." I pretend to roll my shoulder but don't move it more than an inch.

Victor plants his hands on the island, staring at the glittering quartz.

He's not usually this moody. Something's wrong.

I set the glass down. "What? What is it?"

"I know who the mole is," he rasps.

He doesn't have to explain. The mole, the person who infiltrated our family and passed on information to Stephanos. It would have to be someone trusted to get the intel Stephanos seemed to get, intel that kept him one step ahead of us at all times.

Names and faces flit through my head. "Who?" I know I'm not going to like the answer.

"Gino."

I close my eyes and accept this bullet to the heart. My stupid, selfish brother. "That fool." It makes sense. He burned through his trust so quickly. He liked spending money and expected it to come easy. And as the son of one of the top family members, he had access to anything. No one would question his loyalty.

A shadow falls over me. Victor has come around the island to be close to me, and despite my roiling stomach, the hairs on my arms raise a second before he touches me. "Lula, I'm sorry."

"No, you're not." I wrench myself away, wincing as it sets my wounds throbbing. "You're one of them." An enemy. I have to remember that. I keep retreating until I'm a few feet away. "I need to tell my cousin. I need to get out of here." It's stupid to say this to my captor.

He stands at my stool, his hands by his sides, still no expression on his face.

Then he says the unexpected. "And if I let you go? Will you continue on this path to vengeance?"

I'm still reeling from the fact that he would let me go. "What do you care?"

"You belong to me."

"I'm not a possession—" I've stopped retreating. Mistake. Because he's crossed the distance, backing me into the wall. I glare up at him as he sets his hand at my throat.

"You belong to me. And I belong to you." He flexes his hand and releases me. "But you see nothing, consider nothing, but your revenge."

"It's not revenge. It's vengeance. It's for someone else."

"Is it? What does your mother gain by you killing her murderer?"

My chest is rising and falling so rapidly that blood has started trickling down my breast. "She deserves to be avenged."

Victor's face is carved from stone, but his eyes burn like blue lasers. "But does she *require* it?"

"I require it." My voice cracks. He's flaying me open like the sadistic surgeon he is, and I have no more defenses. "They threw her life away. They treated it like nothing. But she wasn't nothing. She was everything."

"And what would she think if she saw you now, her precious daughter? Would she want your life to look like this?"

I suck in a breath. Victor could not have hurt me more if he carved my heart out and held it in front of my face, still beating.

"You spent all these years sharpening yourself to a blade and making yourself a bullet in a gun. But you are more, Lula. You can do, can have, more."

"Shut up," I whisper and turn my face away.

The floor creaks as he leaves.

He's making noise on purpose because he so rarely makes a sound, leaving me with bile in my throat and burning eyes.

Victor

The screens in my media room are filled with motion. Spiro, Joe, and the rest moving around the deserted pizzeria. Cars zooming down streets. Workers in Cavalli's, fixing the walls, prepping them to paint.

I ignore them all and fix my eyes on one screen, the most important one. In the black frame, Lula sits on the bed, staring at the wall. She hasn't crumpled yet, but I can tell she wants to. The news about her brother bowed but didn't break her. More proof that her mother's death was ignored by those Vera loved the most.

They threw her life away. They treated it like nothing. But she wasn't nothing. She was everything.

My captive has not cried yet, but her eyes look bruised. I message the doctor to watch over her and leave my media room.

An hour later, I'm across from the dark doors of the abandoned hotel Spiro gave me the address to in a neutral part of town. Here, supposedly, Stephanos left me my money. A black duffel bag of unmarked bills. Whether the money will be accompanied by the man, I cannot say.

Instead of walking in as instructed, I climb the fire escape of a nearby building and get to the roof to scout the area. From here, I can settle into a sniper's perch and look down onto the drop zone. Not that I have a gun.

A few minutes pass. I'm early, but something tells me my client is earlier still.

The moon drifts across the sky. A rat pokes its head out of a hole and inches toward a dumpster.

A match flares in the dark for a second before being snuffed out, but it's enough. The tiny, mean eye of a cigarette remains, burning red gold.

And there he is. Broad shoulders, shaved head.

I wait in the shadows, contemplating my next steps.

15

Lula

VICTOR LEAVES ME ALONE. For hours. Maybe days. I try to break down the door leading to the hallway where he's gone but have no luck. I even try to break into the dungeon. I stand on a stool and poke into the vents, but they're too small to fit more than a hand and covered in a steel grid. I leave it alone, not wanting to mess with the only source of fresh air in my cushy prison.

I have nothing to do but eat the food in the fridge, take the painkillers he left me, and imagine what I'll do to my brother if I get my hands on him.

I refuse to think of Victor. He's nothing to me. He was never more than my captor. My enemy. And if I am a bullet in a gun, a dagger with a poisoned edge, let me maim him. Let me kill him.

I sleep every so often, fitful and restless, dreaming of a

hitman with silver blond hair and shadows under his eyes. At some point, I wake to the door to the long hallway open. But it's a dead end. There's nothing but more locked doors, an attack dummy, and a few knives.

I could carve my wrath into the walls and locked doors. Instead, I practice fighting, only stopping to eat or rest. Without windows or a clock, I don't know if I sleep for years or merely a nap. The bedroom is as dark as an underground bunker. A tomb. I can't think about this too much, or I'll go mad.

I sleep with a knife in my hand. After one particular spell of sleep, I wake up knowing I'm not alone. *He's* standing in the shadows, wearing a dark suit.

I snap to my feet, knife outstretched.

"Ah, you're awake," he says, as if I'm not ready to stab him. "Get dressed." He nods to the foot of the bed, where he's laid out a black dress and long, tan trench coat.

Clothes. For the first time in. . . as long as I've been here.

"Why?"

"I thought you might enjoy going to a party."

"What sort of party?"

"At Cavalli's. You've been there once. Remember?"

I remember the smoke, the bark of the gun. The cool air wafting up my bare legs under the trench coat.

"What's this about?" As soon as I ask, my mind flashes over the possibilities and spits out the most likely explanation. "Stephanos will be there." My voice is flat.

"He might be. He owes me, you see. And I always collect what I'm owed. He wants to meet me." He leans down and straightens the slinky black dress he's laid out for me. "It turns out you're an excellent bargaining chip."

My heart sinks to my feet. Any hope I had that Victor wasn't one of them is stolen away from me.

And then Victor continues to twist the knife. "I told him I had you. At first, he didn't believe me. But then I showed him some footage."

I close my eyes. Of course, he did. How much footage does he have of me bound, caged, naked, and whipped? My greatest enemy, seeing my greatest humiliation. I could puke.

"And now he says he'll meet with me... on the condition that I bring you to him."

I want to stab him in the eye. I could do it if I were stronger, faster. If my opponent wasn't Victor.

"So that's it?" My chest is heaving, stretching the barely healed marks on my breast. Marks that mean nothing. "You're just going to hand me over?"

"Of course not. You belong to me." His eyes flicker to the bandage above my breast. He cut me like a schoolboy carves his name into a desk. But that doesn't mean he owns me.

One day, he'll find that out.

"Stephanos will not touch you."

I scoff. "That's supposed to reassure me?"

Victor comes closer, his pale eyes pinning me into place. His hand grabs my wrist and presses a point that makes my fingers spasm, and I drop the knife.

He catches it and holds it up. It all happened in a flash, too fast for me to see.

"I have much to teach you. But this time together is at its end. There's a decision for you to make." He tosses the knife so it flips overhead and embeds itself in the wall above the headboard, where it quivers. It's in the dead center of the room, and I half expect the bed to split in half, bisected by this moment and the blade. When it doesn't, I turn back to my nemesis. He looms over me, half of his face in the light and half in shadow. But when he speaks, I hear both the iced-over tones of the psychopath and echoes of the soft, hopeful murmur of a lover.

"So now, I must ask. Lula... will you trust me?"

Victor

Joe drives us to the restaurant, and Lula sits next to me in the back seat, a black silk blindfold over her eyes. When I guided her to take her first steps outside, she raised her head to the sun. She's thinner than when I first brought her here, but not by much. I tried to feed her well, but she's more hardened. The circles under her eyes are darker from a lack of vitamin D, but also not enough feasting with friends and family—not enough joy.

I can't give her everything, even if I wanted to. But maybe I can give her enough.

She said yes to trusting me. But she didn't bother to keep the derision out of her tone. But she is here, next to me, sitting up straight and gorgeous in the sleek black dress I gave her. I can only hope that there's a tiny sliver of trust in her toward me. Maybe there is.

And maybe we are both lying to ourselves.

Joe pulls right up to the door, and I help her out. She wrinkles her nose, probably smelling the stale cigarettes that stain the evening air. Once inside, the smell is better, replaced with butter and garlic. Spiro had a hand in hiring new people for the kitchen, and the result is a massive improvement over what Cavalli's used to be.

The decor still has the same faded carpet and old furniture. But there's a fresh coat of paint and no sign of bullet holes. I pull Lula along to the back room, pausing in the shadowy hallway to lift the blindfold from her eyes.

She blinks once and takes in her surroundings with the wary look of a hunter in unknown territory.

Low laughter and the murmur of men's voices come from the room ahead.

"Ready?" I ask.

She shrugs and visibly hardens. I draw her close on the pretense of fiddling with the coat's collar.

"Do this for me," I whisper in her ear. "And I will give you everything you want and more." I pull away to take in her expression, but it's blank and remote. It reminds me of my own face in the mirror.

Maybe I taught her more than I should have.

"You're missing one thing." She's wearing my tan trench coat, and I reach into a pocket to pull out a silver tube of lipstick. Her lips compress to hold back a grimace, but she lets me paint it on her. A pop of red in her colorless face. Warpaint. "Now you're ready."

"You're not going to tie me up?" She holds up her hands, presenting her wrists.

"I think you'll behave. The stakes are too high, the reward too great."

Her eyebrows twitch, but her forehead smooths before I can ask about her thoughts. "Let's get this over with."

"As you wish." I lead her into the room where she faced Stephanos last. According to Spiro, it's much the same with the unneeded tables and chairs pushed to the side. A few men lounge around the long table lining the opposite wall, and they fall silent as we approach.

"Lucrezia Romano, meet my new friends. Spiro, Uzi, Kill Zone." Each man stands as I name them. There are five more newcomers, all vetted and vouched for by Spiro. He completes the introductions by saying, "And Joe's out back. He's coming in soon."

Lula stands silent through this, shifting slightly from foot to foot. I keep a hand on her elbow.

"Shall we?" I sweep a hand toward the table, and the men part to make a path for us. I guide her to settle in the center of the booth lining the wall. The seat of honor, but hemmed in on either side by me and Spiro.

"NICE TO MEET YA, MS. ROMANO," Kill Zone says after a nervous glance at me.

She nods, her jaw still rigid. She's trying to figure out what's happening. There's no sign of Stephanos. Or Bruno.

She sits with her hands in her lap, the long sleeves of my coat draped past her fingertips. I didn't offer to take the coat; she might feel safer in it, less exposed. And I like seeing her in my clothes. It's a big change from the last time she walked in here wearing my coat. Now, no one looks at her bare body but me.

The back door opens and squeals closed. Everyone tenses, but it's just Joe. He walks in. "Sorry, I'm late. Business." He gives me a significant look.

Spiro pipes up. "I made sure the kitchen has their orders."

"No trouble?" I ask, resting a hand on Lula's rigid knee.

"Naw. They'll be ready soon." He picks up a wine bottle and uncorks it. "Something to drink while we wait?"

Lula doesn't move, but I nod to her wine glass. He leans in to fill it, and the men around us relax a little. There's still a readiness, an air of anticipation, but a few of them light cigarettes or take a sip of their drinks. Uzi relinquishes his hold on his gun and sets it on the floor, letting it lean against his chair.

One of the newcomers cocks his head at Kill Zone. "Kill Zone? That's your name?"

"That's what they call me." Kill Zone shrugs. "I'm thinking of shortening it to Killz."

"Killz?" Spiro snorts. "Isn't that the stuff my ma had us paint the bathroom with? For mold?"

"Yeah," says Kill Zone.

A raspy sandpaper sound echoes as Joe scratches his stubbly chin. "That shit is great."

A server appears at the main entrance, pushing a food cart. A huge dish covered by a silver dome rests on top. Everyone's eyes snap to it. The server is a young man with a long neck whose Adam's apple bobs as he swallows. Under the red stain of acne, his skin is blanched pale.

"I got it," Joe says, snubbing out his cigarette and heading to take over controlling the cart. The server relinquishes it, and Joe pushes it right in front of Lula and me. "Go ahead," I gesture to her. "The main course. I sourced it myself."

Suppressing a frown, she reaches for it. Hesitates. With visible willpower, she lifts the silver dome.

For a few moments, she stares at the contents of the dish. Even though he knew about it beforehand, Spiro sucks in a shocked breath. Kill Zone and Uzi mutter quiet curses. One of the men, a newcomer whose name I already forgot, staggers to the corner to quietly retch.

Behind the cart, Joe is looking away.

But not Lula. Her eyes feast on the gruesome sight. Then she slowly lowers the silver dome to cover the severed head of Bruno, Stephanos' right-hand man. It's not as gory as it could have been. After I cornered and garrotted him, I let much of the blood drain away.

Lula twists to look up at me. She's flushed and breathing hard like she's run up the stairs but trying to control her emotions. I can see the question in her eyes. *Why?*

"Excuse us," I say. "We need a moment."

Lula

Victor ushers me into a dark room. A flick of the lights and I see it's a bathroom. In case I have to throw up?

A quick inventory tells me I'm not queasy but numb. I brace my hands on the bathroom sink just in case. The place is cleaner than it used to be. Not what I expected, but nothing about today is.

I expected Victor to parade me in front of Stephanos, to put me on display like a trained submissive. I expected torture or humiliation.

Nothing could've prepared me for the sight of a man's head on a platter. Victor stands behind me, much like he did the first time we fucked in his bathroom. I meet his eyes in the mirror. There's no color in my face other than my red, red lips. "You could've warned me."

"Would you have believed me?"

"Hell no." I shake my head. This isn't my reality. I have no idea what's going on. "You killed Bruno." At least, I think that was Bruno. It wasn't easy to recognize the slack features, but the shaved head was huge. And who else could it be?

Victor doesn't deny it, so I can move on to my next question. "Why?"

"Because he shot at you," Victor growls. The tops of his cheekbones flush as bright as my lips. "He almost killed you. You could've died."

"I thought. . ." I thought a lot of things. "I thought you were going to. . ." I don't know what to say, so I stop talking.

Victor turns me to face him. He's a beautiful, brutal force of nature. A blizzard. An oncoming iceberg. I don't understand him, but he's always been honest about who he is. "I told you to trust me, and I'd give you everything. I had to prove it to you. This is my proof."

I gape at him, my jaw hanging toward the floor. So I ask again, "Why?"

"You know why. You're it for me." His touch on my cheek is gentle, but I startle. "I don't know what love is. I do know I would slaughter every man and woman on Earth and serve their heads to you on a platter on the chance it would make you smile."

Mass murder. How romantic. "That's not. . . don't do that." I'm still trying to wrap my head around the fact that he doesn't want to destroy me.

He pushes closer, crowding me against the sink, and presses something into my hand. A knife. I automatically settle it into the proper grip.

"Don't you understand?" He takes my hand and brings the knife up to his own throat. "I'd let you cut my own heart out if you wanted."

His hand falls away, and for a moment, I keep the blade against his pretty, pale skin.

I could do it. I could kill him.

He speaks again, and I have to lessen the pressure against his throat so I don't cut him. "I had to prove I'm worthy of you before you'd trust me. Love me."

I have to stop myself from saying, "I don't love you."

Because Victor has taught me not to lie. Not to him. Not to myself.

My hand flexes, and I press the knife too hard. A thin cut appears, and blood streams down. I set down the knife and cover the wound, trying to stem the flood. "Oh. Oh no. . ."

He captures my hand, not noticing or caring about the cut. "Lucrezia. My love. Tell me what you want from me, and I'll make it happen. The gang out there"—he tips his head out the door—"is yours to command. Or I'll kill them all." He says it with such ease I flinch. He cups my cheek, blood still streaming down the hollow of his throat. It's a shallow cut, but it's bleeding so much. If Victor's aware of it, he doesn't care.

He strokes his thumb over my cheekbone. "I'd kill everyone in the world if you wanted." He sounds so happy, it's disturbing. "Say the word. Cut my throat right now, and I'd be happy because it's you, Lula. It will always be you."

My breath is rattling in and out of me. My throat was lined with poisoned knives, but they're gone now. My chest still aches, like nothing will soothe it, but. . .

I push up to tiptoe, pulling his head down so I can reach his lips. He grips the lapels of the coat I'm wearing, drawing me up so his mouth can dominate mine.

We kiss until I'm surging against him; the ache in me spreads through my core to my limbs.

He takes my shoulders and pushes us slightly apart, keeping a bare millimeter between us. "Death or belonging to me. Those are your options."

"Your death or mine?" I raise my head to murmur against his lips.

"I don't want to live in this world alone. Without you, Lula, I might as well be dead."

I draw back. The nick at his throat really is making a

mess. I curse and find a paper towel to clean it up. He holds still and lets me, watching me with a tenderness that makes me ache.

Fates preserve us. There might be a small part of me that loves him. And that is enough.

But first things first.

I straighten and toss the bloody paper towel into the trash. Then I pick up the knife, testing its weight in my palm. "Where's Stephanos?"

"Hiding like the rat he is. Do you want me to take you to him?"

"Yes."

He smiles and takes my hand. The one without the knife. "Then let's go."

16

Lula

THE DRIVE LEAVING Cavalli's is very different from the one a mere hour before.

This time, I relax in the backseat with Victor, holding his hand. No blindfold. I returned his knife, and he gave me back my Sig Sauer. Its weight feels weird but familiar.

Two of the guys ride in the front. Joe and Spiro. Joe is driving again, keeping to back roads.

We're rolling down an alleyway when I recognize the silver siding of the building up ahead.

"Stop here a moment," I say. "Please."

Joe looks into the rearview mirror, and Victor nods. The car slows to a stop.

The back door of Three Diner opens before I step out of the car. Two of the owners greet me. The tall young woman with dark glasses and the tiny white-haired one with weathered hands. The shadow of a third woman, round and matronly, haunts the door.

"You've returned," the young woman says, with a hint of a smile. Her head angles like she's looking into the sky or hearing music playing far away. "And you're not alone."

"Yes." I don't know what I want to say to them, so I wait through an awkward pause.

"You're ready, daughter of Vera," the white-haired lady pronounces.

My throat clogs up, but I nod.

"Then go, and fate will bless you."

I slide into the back seat, and Joe takes his foot off the brake a second later. Victor tips his head to the two women and gives them a cocky wave.

As soon as they're out of view, he leans forward to study my face. "Did you get what you needed?"

"Yes," I say, but then I amend, "but not from them. I already have what I need."

"Almost," he says and holds up a silver chain, the sword charm dangling from his palm.

I'd cuss him out, but I'm too happy to see my old necklace. I lift my hair and let him put it on me. He takes his sweet time and fiddles with it so the sword settles on my sternum.

And all too soon, we're at an ancient brick warehouse a few blocks away from the docks. I recognize the area. "This is Vesuvi territory."

"Yes. Stephanos has bolt holes like this all over the city. It's how he's survived." He's patting his clothes, presumably checking his hidden knives. "He's inside."

This is it. The moment I've prepared for all my life.

I press the sword into my skin for a second before shrugging out of Victor's long coat. I take a moment to check my Glock. In the front seat, Joe and Spiro are doing the same.

"Here." Victor holds up a black vest. I shrug it on, and he makes sure it's fastened up the front.

"We disabled those cameras," Spiro tells me, pointing to the surrounding buildings and the silver or black equipment nestled in the eaves. "But he'll have more inside."

"Thank you."

A heaviness settles over me, more than the weight of the vest. Reality descending. I open the car door, and the sky above is so blue, I could cry. The shadows at my feet are dark and deep, and I can see every speck of dust floating in the air between me and the warehouse door.

When I step out of the car, Victor appears at my side. "I'm coming with you."

"Of course." He's made it clear he wants to keep me close. Whether because he loves me or thinks I'm his property, it doesn't matter.

He pulls on a black ski mask and glides ahead of me. Signaling me to wait, he presses a hand to the heavy steel door. It opens easily, without a sound. Did he come here beforehand and oil the hinges? I wouldn't be surprised.

Victor leans in, his whisper barely stirring my hair. "He's fond of booby traps, but there won't be many here because he hasn't had the time to set them. He was hiding elsewhere. Recent events flushed him out."

Recent events. Like Victor killing Bruno and presenting his head to me on a platter. A grisly valentine.

I can't help it. I glance at Victor with a little grin. He lifts his hone-blond brows and signals me. *Come?*

In answer, I press a thumb and forefinger together and stalk into the warehouse, gripping my Glock tight. The safety's off, and it leads the way. The vest Victor gave me lays like a stone on my chest, but I welcome the weight. It keeps my heart from flying from my chest.

But I'm calm and centered as I move deeper into my enemy's hiding place.

I don't need luck or fate.

I have Victor.

Once inside, he signals me to go left. There's a TV buzzing somewhere off to the right, but I trust him. A quick glance at the concrete floor shows faint footprints in the dust and a glint of steel wire.

Booby trap number one.

We round a huge shipping container, and I stop when he signals me to.

He points at a camera overhead. We back up and find a different way through the stacked crates and past a few big machines folded up like the carcasses of giant dead insects. Victor points out more cameras, another trip wire—booby trap number two—and a patch of disturbed dust that seems to cover a metal plate of some sort. Every step of the way, he uses the hand signals he taught me during my captivity to guide me safely forward. We sidle carefully past booby trap number three, all while an announcer on TV narrates a baseball game.

We've taken care not to kick up too much dust, but it hangs thick in the air. I breathe through my mouth, willing myself not to sneeze.

The TV noise is coming from a small room up ahead. Once an overseer's office, the grimy windows mute the yellow light, but it glows like a beacon of light and sound in the forgotten space. There's a set of footprints leading from it to the back of the warehouse, to an exit or bathroom or both. Victor and I creep around until we're in front of the door. Through it, we have a straight line of sight into the cramped room. There's a shelf with a microwave on top and a mini fridge below. Takeout containers and potato chip bags litter the floor. Just out of sight, on a sagging couch, Stephanos lounges in ratty slippers.

He's just sitting there in his sweatpants, watching TV and eating chips. Living his life long after he snuffed my mother's out.

Victor, slowly so I can see him, draws a long knife. A good throwing knife. He mimes tossing it at one of the booby traps behind us. The noise will startle Stephanos and drive him out of his nest.

Right into the line of fire.

I nod and raise my Glock. Victor slips forward, and I bite back a hiss. He's sneaking closer to get a better shot at hitting the booby trap but also to cover any other hidden exits Stephanos might use. My instinct is to call him back and tell him to stop, but I don't.

I trust him.

He raises the knife and pauses. I reaffirm my grip on my gun.

His throw is so quick and smooth I don't see the knife. But the instant it hits the trip wire, there's a discordant twang, and a tower of boxes comes crashing down.

Stephanos is up and racing out the door toward me. His yellow-white shirt fills my vision, and I brace myself and take aim.

Crack!

The force of the shot reverberates up my arm. Acrid smoke fills my nose. I fire again and again, my ears deafened by the noise. The pulse of the gun is a steady heartbeat against my palm. In the distance, through the gray clouds, Stephanos jerks and dances.

There's a clap of noise and an explosion of heat that

sends me staggering to the right. The world is muted beyond my buzzing ears.

Something else knocks into me, and I crash to the floor. The weight isn't sharp or too heavy, and I understand what it is as the dust settles. Victor. Covering me with his huge body.

He's on his feet in the next second, peeling me off the floor and backing me into a safe corner. I keep my Glock out, pointing into the dancing dust cloud at his back. Covering him like he covered me.

My back hits a corner, and a breath escapes. The warehouse area we're in is wrecked, with clouds of sawdust threatening to make me cough and debris littering the floor.

"Stephanos?" I manage to say without hacking on the heavy particulate hanging in the air.

"Hurt, but he managed to trigger the explosion." He pauses, and we both hear it: a labored wheezing a few yards away.

The hunt is not over yet.

Victor helps me step over splintered wood and creep closer to our quarry.

Stephanos is a slight form on the floor, grunting as he tries to pull his leg out from under a fallen steel beam. Trapped by the explosion he triggered.

I pause and look up at Victor, waiting for his signal. His ski mask is no longer black but gray with dust.

After a sweep, he raises his hand and touches his forefinger to his thumb, giving me the go-ahead.

I raise my hand and offer him my Glock. He understands instantly and trades my Glock for his knife.

For a moment, we stand together, holding our weapons and gazing into each other's eyes. His gaze drops to my lips like he wishes he could kiss me. My body tightens. *Okay*, I signal back.

He touches my back gently. *Go.*

I step over a fallen board and stroll to the spot where Stephanos is pinned.

He's smaller up close. Grooves line his face and sunken cheeks, surrounding his black, beady eyes. There's an unhealthy pallor to his skin, and I know that time and heart disease would've ended him sooner rather than later.

But that won't be his fate.

His eyes go wide, and he bares his teeth when he sees me. "You."

"Me." I sink down and plant a knee on his chest.

He blinks at me with sawdust-coated eyelashes. Up close and exposed like this, his ugliness is repulsive, like something crawling out from under a rock. He bats at me, but his arms are limp, weakened by the bullets he took to the chest. He struggles to breathe under my weight, his body fighting to stay alive.

I set the knife at his grime-streaked throat, ready to strike the way Victor took pains to teach me. "This is for my mother."

Victor

The blade flashes as Lula cuts just as I taught her. I force myself to wait with my weight pitched forward into my toes until the stench of death rises in the air. I pull off my ski mask, meant to dull my distinctive hair.

Lula rises slowly, her dark hair swinging like a cape

behind her. I don't have to go to her. She returns to me, offering me the knife back. Her eyes are black. "You're right. It is more satisfying."

There's blood on her jaw and cheek. I secrete away the knife and touch her face carefully, tipping it this way and that. There's a dark stain in the corner of her mouth, blending with the brighter red of her lipstick. "You have some blood. . ."

"Don't worry," she murmurs. "It's not mine."

I swipe it away and bow to claim her lips.

My dark, vengeful angel.

The sound of a slamming door breaks us apart. "What —" She raises her empty hands. I still have her Glock.

"It's all right," I say, even as I draw us into the shadows. "Spiro made a call to your cousin."

"Royal?" she says as her cousin appears, flushed and angry and glaring at me. His men fan out behind him, covering him.

"Lula." His gaze sweeps the area, registering Stephanos' still form before returning to us. He opens his mouth, but before he can speak, someone else pushes forward, raising a gun with a shout.

~

Lula

I WATCH it in slow motion. Royal, looking angry and relieved, ready to tear me a new one. Enzo and the rest of our cousins are covering his back but turn toward the new threat.

It's my brother, crashing through the debris, his gaze

fixed on Victor. "You," he snarls and swings his gun muzzle upward.

"No," I shout and step between them.

Too late.

Gino's pulling the trigger, but fate's on our side. In his carelessness, Gino blundered into one of the booby traps. He's already falling forward as the gun goes off. I flinch, but the shot goes wild. It hits a machine and ricochets. Everyone ducks.

Royal curses in Italian. "Someone take his gun."

Enzo rushes to take care of it. Gino's still flailing on the floor.

"Idiota." Royal runs a hand over his face. He looks tired as he turns to me. "Lucrezia."

"I'm okay." I step forward, tears pricking my eyes at the sight of him. "I'm in a vest. Victor. . ." I turn back to where Victor stands silently, the sunlight filtering in through the dust gilds his stunning features. He looks calm, maybe a little sad.

Behind me, Royal clears his throat, and I realize I've lost my train of thought. It's not often that that happens.

"Victor," I say more firmly, "found Stephanos. He helped me."

"Helped you?"

"Saved me. He saved me." From myself especially.

Royal looks back and forth between us. I can tell it's on the tip of his tongue to give the order to incapacitate or maybe even kill Victor.

So I gesture for my beautiful monster to come and wait until he's standing at my side to make things clear. "You can't kill him," I tell Royal and the men of my family, gripping Victor's hand. "He's mine."

17

L*ula*

The Regis mansion is the heart of La Famiglia. Dark and filled with heavy, imposing furniture, it's a shocking contrast to the sterile, modern decor Victor prefers. Royal used to keep the temperature five degrees cooler than what was comfortable, but then he found his wife. Now, the air is a tad too warm but perfect for Leah and the spaghetti strap camisoles she likes to wear. And if she gets overheated while baking, sliding things in and out of the oven, well, Royal's always trying to get her naked, anyway.

There was a day when I swore that Royal would never marry for love. Some would say he didn't, but I know better. When it comes to devious, dangerous men, love looks a lot like obsession.

I lean on a sturdy mahogany leather chair, studying my cousin's dark expression and sipping my wine. I refused any food—my stomach is still unsettled—but accepted a glass of merlot. It's still not as good as the wine Victor keeps for me.

Royal and I have caught up on a lot of things in the past hour. Family, business, Gino's betrayal, Stephanos' death, and the way Victor turned his gang. We're in agreement on many things, but—

"So you're telling me I have to accept this murderer into my family?"

"Yes." I toy with the sword charm on my necklace. My mother bought it to give to me when I turned thirteen, and I used to feel her presence whenever I touched it. Now, the miniature blade reminds me of Victor.

Royal shakes his head, muttering in Italian.

"He's a useful asset. But even if he wasn't. . ." I shrug. "I want him." I gave up everything for vengeance. It's time I claimed something for myself.

"If he betrays you. . ."

"He won't. Any more than you could betray Leah."

Royal accepts this with a growl, and I hide my smile. One day, I'll tell him my theory on how much he and Victor are alike.

"I'll allow it," Royal says finally. "On one condition." He digs in his pocket and holds up a dull silver coin. On it, a long-haired man stands with his head bowed, holding a cross. Or is it a woman holding a sword?

"You've offered this to me before." I didn't take it because I'd just met David. And because Royal was still solidifying his power base, ushering the old guard out and replacing them with new, well-trained men who wouldn't mind taking orders from a woman. From me.

"It's time." He presses it into my hand. For such a small thing, it's heavy, carrying the weight of the Regis family.

"Accepted. Although, with Gino out, there's an extra seat." When Victor proves himself, he'd be perfect for it.

"Don't push it."

I turn with a smirk. "If that's all, then I'd like to see Victor."

"No more disappearing," Royal says. He's pretending my time in captivity was by choice. Like an extended vacation. It's probably easier for him to think of it that way. It's not as if he didn't do the same thing to Leah.

"No."

Royal downs his drink in one swallow and sets the glass down. He moves around the desk to flank me but doesn't stop me. "And I can make it official? To the Family?"

"Yes. I'm already acting as the family attorney; I might as well be in truth." I stop and face him and let him take my face in his hands and kiss my cheeks.

"Then, consigliere, welcome home."

~

"Consigliere?" Victor murmurs as we make our way to the car. Enzo is behind the wheel. Joe, Spiro, and the rest of Stephanos' old gang are still being vetted. But eventually, they'll be brought into the Regis regime. Another one of my acts as second in command of the Regis Family.

"Yes. He's been wanting to make it official for a few months now. It comes with a seat at La Famiglia's table." Royal always took my advice before he voted. But now I have a vote of my own.

"There's another seat free." The one that belonged to my father and then Gino. "Royal isn't ready to fill it, but perhaps if an outsider made himself indispensable to the Family…"

"Then I'm sure I can make myself useful."

I sink into the car. It's not that late, just after sunset, but I'm tired. Royal tried to get us to stay for dinner, threatening to unleash Leah on us, but I negotiated our escape by promising to come back in the morning for brunch.

Victor lets me rest, leaning forward to murmur directions to Enzo.

I must have dozed off because when I open my eyes, the car is pulling up outside the building that houses Victor's penthouse. The one he originally took me to.

The first time, he carried me in. This time, I walk in of my own volition after Victor helps me from the car.

It feels like a lifetime since I've been here. Stephanos is gone. My mother's been avenged. The truth about my brother is out, and he'll be punished. And I may have lost a brother, but I gained a lover. Victor brings a handful of made men with him, along with his own unique skills.

Ultimately, La Famiglia has won.

And I've claimed a victory of my own.

"Where's the dungeon?" I ask Victor as we step into the elevator. I have a theory, but I want him to confirm it.

"In the basement."

I knew it.

He hovers a long finger over the button for the lower floor before he presses the one to take us to the top.

He takes me to the bathroom and positions me in front of the sink. His big hands roam over me, checking for blood, bruises, and tender spots. I took a moment in the bathroom at Royal's mansion to dust off the worst of the wood splinters and debris that coated my dress and hair from the explosion.

The worst of my wounds are carried over from my time in captivity—the letters carved above my heart. When Victor tackled me to protect me from the explosion, I crashed to the ground. The force broke the fragile skin, and the letters he carved were bleeding again.

I pull down the dress's square neckline and push my sword necklace aside so Victor can remove the dirty bandage. He growls as he fusses over the marks.

"You're the one who did this to me." I roll my eyes at his muttered curses. "It'll heal." I stop him before he covers the cuts with another bandage. "Wait. Let me see something."

I point to the letters carved into my chest. The V is the easiest letter to read. Next to it, in the same size script, is the letter R.

I studied them when Victor left me but didn't understand. The V is obvious: V for Victor. But the second letter... "R? What's your last name?"

"I have none," he says. "Not anymore. I figured I could take yours."

I drop my hand, my arm muscles suddenly too weak to hold it up. "Romano?"

"Or Regis. Your mother was a Regis, correct?"

"She was."

"And here I am, part of the Regis family. If you and your cousin will have me."

"He will accept you." He will if I have any say in it.

"You saved me from him." His touch is tender on my cheek.

"Yes." I turn fully and rise to tiptoes to thread my arms around his broad shoulders. I pull him down until his lips brush mine and whisper, "If anyone is going to kill you, it's going to be me."

He straightens, lifting me off my feet as he claims my

mouth. His kiss is ice and fire, and I savor the solid power of him, rubbing my swelling breasts against his chest. His dick jabs my thigh.

He swivels and sets me on the bathroom counter. I'm already spreading my legs. The dress he gave me was form-fitting but modest enough, with a hem that ends an inch above my knee. I wriggle, trying to pull it up, but it's too tight and doesn't budge. Until Victor helps by ripping it in half so it's open to my navel.

"Yes," I gasp and scoot forward to the edge of the counter. I'm not wearing underwear. He didn't give me any earlier today, and after spending so long naked, a bra and panties would feel weird.

Victor's already opened his pants. The head of his cock is red and angry, dripping pre-cum. He finds my sopping wet entrance and pushes in an inch. I'm squirming, trying to stretch to accommodate him when he digs his hand into my hair to hold me still.

"I will give you everything," he promises. In one swift move, he pushes inside, spearing me as he wrenches my head back. Bombs explode in my brain. I cum right then, shaking in his grip. He watches me with his icy gaze.

"Krasiva. Mi kama." He cups my bottom and lifts me so he can sink even deeper, filling the depths of me. My insides stretch around him, slowly accommodating his girth, but nothing can help me get used to his length. At this angle, pressed against him with gravity pulling me down, the head of his cock is knocking on my cervix.

I tear at his shirt collar, sending buttons flying as I rip the dress shirt open so I can fasten my mouth to his neck. I find the cut I made and suck on it, hard. His growl rolls through me, the delicious vibrations making me pulse around him.

"Fuck, Lula. You will be the end of me."

That's the idea. I sink my fingers into his hair, bare my teeth, and nip at the vein stretching from his neck to his shoulder. His winter scent swirls around me. Before I can bite him fully, he tugs my head up by my hair, and the sting in my scalp is enough to make me cum again.

Victor's voice rings savagely in my ears as I convulse, squeezing down on his dick like the orgasm turned my inner muscles into a vice. He sets me back on the counter, pulling out. His shirt's torn open, his hair disheveled from my fists, and there's a red mark on his neck from my teeth. His own mouth is contorted into a snarl. He doesn't look like we've been making love. He looks like he's been in a fight.

He backs away slowly, his dick bobbing in the air. *Come*, he gestures, and I do, stalking after him, further tearing my dress so I can strip it off as I go. Naked in nothing but stilettos, I wait until he's reached the bedroom before dropping to my knees. I crawl on all fours, my body swaying sinuously all the way to the bedroom. My breasts swing, the necklace dangling between them. I keep my head up and my gaze on Victor so I can savor the blue flame burning in his eyes. I prowl like an animal on the hunt, like an obedient pet, like a submissive safe in her Dom's control. My humiliation and his happiness are a delicious heat that warms me through and through.

He sits on the end of the bed to wait for me, pulling off his shirt and baring his chest. Miles of pale, sculpted muscle, pretty enough to make Michelangelo weep. I crawl to him, mouth watering at the sight of him and his gorgeous dick, but I don't get to play. As I'm reaching for his cock, he wraps his hand around my neck and pulls me up to meet his mouth. His fingers dig into my throat as his lips sear mine, whispering promises of pain and pleasure. My body aches, my gaze darkening until I'm blind with need for him.

I push on his shoulders so he lies back on the bed, and I climb him. Bracing my palms on his hard pectoral muscles, I set my entrance over his erection and plunge down.

My necklace bounces as I ride him.

His hand collars my throat, controlling my movements even as I'm on top. "Mi kama. My weapon. My sharp-tongued sword. Fate forged you for me."

"A sheath for the dagger. A dagger for the sheath."

"You belong to me." He snaps his hips, driving into my depths.

"Yes." I rock over him, accepting the pain as he batters my insides. I dig my nails into his pale shoulders, willing to scratch him bloody. "And you to me. Because. . ." I hesitate, the words so sharp, so real, they cut. My heart aches like a bruise.

But Victor shows no mercy. "Say it."

"I love you." And it's the truth.

~

THANK you for reading Victor and Lucrezia's story! I have more Mafia Brides books planned.

In the meantime, read Royal and Leah's book, Revenge is Sweet and grab the exclusive extra story, A Bun in the Oven, here.

And let me know if you want more mafia brides! I have some ideas cooking...

Love and blood-soaked poniards,

Lee Savino

FREE BOOK

My dark lumberjack romance, Beauty & the Lumberjacks, is free right now for newsletter subscribers

Grab it here: https://BookHip.com/WZLTMQX

Beauty & the Lumberjacks

After this logging season, I'm never having sex again. Because: *reasons*.

But first, I have a gig earning room and board and ten thousand dollars by 'entertaining' eight lumberjacks. **Eight strong and strapping Paul Bunyan types, big enough to break me in two.**

There's Lincoln, the leader, the stern, silent type...

Jagger, the Kurt Cobain look-alike, with a soul full of music and rockstar moves...

Elon & Oren, ginger twins who share everything...

Saint, the quiet genius with a monster in his pants...

Roy and Tommy, who just want to watch...

And Mason, who hates me and won't say why, but on his night tries to break me with pleasure...

They own me: body, mind and orgasms.

But when they discover my secret—the reason I'm hiding from the world—everything changes.

AUTHOR BIO - LEE SAVINO

Lee Savino has plans to take over the world, but most days can't find her keys or her phone, so she just stays home and writes smexy (smart + sexy) romance. She loves chocolate, lives in yoga pants, and looks great in hats.

For tons of crazy fun, join her Goddess Group on Facebook or visit www.leesavino.com to sign up for her mailing list and get a free book.

Website: www.leesavino.com

Facebook: Goddess Group: https://www.facebook.com/groups/LeeSavino/

ALSO BY LEE SAVINO - ALL BOOKS SEPARATE LINKS

Want more dark romance? Check out the Innocence Trilogy written with Stasia Black. Start with Innocence: dark mafia romance.

Dark Mafia Romance

Mafia Brides
Revenge is Sweet
Vengeance is Mine

A Dark Mafia Romance trilogy with Stasia Black
Innocence
Awakening
Queen of the Underworld

Beauty and the Rose trilogy with Stasia Black
Beauty's Beast
Beauty & the Thorns
Beauty & the Rose

Contemporary Romance

Royal Bad Boy
Royally Fake Fiancé

Beauty & The Lumberjacks
Her Marine Daddy
Her Dueling Daddies

Paranormal romance

Berserker Saga
Sold to the Berserkers
Mated to the Berserkers
Bred by the Berserkers (FREE novella only available at www.leesavino.com)
Taken by the Berserkers
Given to the Berserkers
Claimed by the Berserkers
Rescued by the Berserker
Captured by the Berserkers
Kidnapped by the Berserkers
Bonded to the Berserkers
Berserker Babies
Night of the Berserkers
Owned by the Berserkers
Tamed by the Berserkers
Mastered by the Berserkers
Surrendered to the Berserkers

Berserker Warriors
Aegir
Siebold with Ines Johnson

Bad Boy Alphas with Renee Rose
Alpha's Temptation

Alpha's Danger
Alpha's Prize
Alpha's Challenge
Alpha's Obsession
Alpha's Desire
Alpha's War
Alpha's Mission
Alpha's Bane
Alpha's Secret
Alpha's Prey
Alpha's Sun

Shifter Ops with Renee Rose
Alpha's Moon
Alpha's Vow
Alpha's Revenge
Alpha's Fire
Alpha's Rescue
Alpha's Command

Midnight Doms with Renee Rose
Alpha's Blood
His Captive Mortal
All Souls Night

Sci fi romance

Planet of Kings with Tabitha Black
Brutal Mate
Brutal Claim
Brutal Capture

Brutal Beast
Brutal Demon

Tsenturion Warriors with Golden Angel
Alien Captive
Alien Tribute
Alien Abduction

Dragons in Exile with Lili Zander
Draekon Mate
Draekon Fire
Draekon Heart
Draekon Abduction
Draekon Destiny
Daughter of Draekons
Draekon Fever
Draekon Rogue
Draekon Holiday

Draekon Rebel Force with Lili Zander
Draekon Warrior
Draekon Conqueror
Draekon Pirate
Draekon Warlord
Draekon Guardian

Cowboy Romance

Wild Whip Ranch with Tristan River
Cowboy's Babygirl
Taming His Wild Girl

Made in the USA
Columbia, SC
15 July 2024

38377685R00117